TRANSPORTED

The adventures
of Thomas
and Claire

Paul Hankins

TRANSPORTED

Copyright © 2013 by Paul Hankins

Illustrations by David Coates
Cover photograph by Maureen Nicholson

Visit the authors website at www.paulsbooks.ca.

ISBN: 978-1-77069-511-5

Word Alive Press
131 Cordite Road, Winnipeg, MB R3W 1S1
www.wordalivepress.ca

WORD ALIVE PRESS
Just Write!

Library and Archives Canada Cataloguing in Publication

Hankins, Paul, 1956-
        Transported : the adventures of Thomas
and Claire / Paul Hankins.
ISBN 978-1-77069-511-5

        I. Title.

PS8615.A5543T73 2012   jC813'.6   C2012-901786-8

To my own Four Heroes, all eight of them.

acknowledgements

Without the encouragement of my longsuffering wife, Brenda, this story might still be just an idea. I'm also grateful to my sister Peggy for her steady, candid critique. And thank you to the many others who read chapters, raised their eyebrows, and provided much-appreciated feedback.

chapter 1

"Thomas. Thom–mas. Thomm–maas! Where are you, Thomas? It's lunchtime!"

Claire stood on the back porch calling for her brother. She knew he wasn't far away because she'd seen him outside the kitchen window just a moment before. She went back in the house, put down her book, slipped on her shoes, then came outside and looked for Thomas in the most likely place—the garage.

He was there, all right, making something out of a small block of wood, two eggbeaters, and an assortment of radio parts. Today he was building a "Transporter." His creation was almost as big as a loaf of bread.

Thomas had spent a dollar at a garage sale for the eggbeaters and attached them to one end of the wooden block. On the other end he glued a magnet from a car speaker and then fastened a sparkplug between the eggbeaters. His dad had thrown the car speaker and sparkplug in the trash that morning and Thomas was pleased he'd found them before the garbage truck came by. He carved out a space in the block of wood for two batteries and connected them with a piece of wire to a radio button.

Thomas often created machines and gizmos and pretended they could do special things, like shoot down alien spaceships. The Transporter was almost finished when Claire walked into the garage.

"Thomas, it's lunchtime," she said. "Didn't you hear me calling you?"

Thomas kept working. Claire stared at him for a minute, then frowned.

"By the way, do you know where my bicycle is?" she asked.

Thomas didn't say anything. He didn't even look up. He scratched his armpit, then picked up a screwdriver.

"Thomas..." demanded Claire. "Thomas!"

She waited a moment, a scowl growing across her face.

"Yeah?" he answered slowly, not sounding too interested.

Claire looked at what he was making. She sneered and brushed her long blonde ponytail off her shoulders.

"There's two things I don't understand about eleven-year-old boys: why they play so much hockey and why they have to waste their time making things that never actually do anything."

There was a pause, then Thomas spoke. "And why do thirteen-year-old girls spend hours sitting around reading dumb books... and never remember where they leave their stuff?"

"I left my bike right here in the garage yesterday, and it's not here now."

"No, it's beside the garage because it was in my way and I moved it out."

"Oh you!" snapped Claire. "Why are you so... so irritating?"

This, of course, was a rhetorical question which Thomas ignored. He tightened a screw on his Transporter, then held it in the air, nodding slowly.

"There." He smiled with satisfaction, pushing his

tussled hair from his eyes. He examined the Transporter closely. "Say, Claire," he said without lifting his eyes, "how would you like to travel someplace far away?"

Claire's bottom lip jutted out. She crossed her arms, took two steps forward, grabbed the Transporter from Thomas' hands, and ran out onto the driveway.

"And how would you like to see this stupid thing travel someplace far away?" she exclaimed.

Thomas was close behind. Claire brought her arm back to throw the Transporter over the fence into the neighbours' yard when Thomas caught up and clutched her arm.

"Give that back right now!" he yelled. "You'll wreck it. Give it back! I'm telling! Give it!"

Claire took the Transporter in her other hand and held it above her head. She was sometimes embarrassed at being tall for her age, but not now. She had no problem keeping the Transporter away from Thomas. She spun around, amused by her shorter brother's frenzied efforts to get it back, like a frantic dog jumping at a doggie biscuit just out of reach.

"What do you call this wonderful contraption?" she asked, her voice raised in mock interest.

"It's my Transporter. Now give it!"

"A Transporter. Amazing! And what, exactly, does a Transporter do?"

"It's for traveling places. Now give it to me before you break it!"

Claire recognized the radio button on the side of the Transporter. With a teasing tone, she said, "Oh! And don't tell me you can listen to your favourite radio station while you travel? Unbelievable! How convenient!"

"That's the Activator. Don't touch it!"

"The Activator? Of course! I should have known. All Transporters come with an Activator, don't they?"

The sparkplug and speaker magnet suddenly shook loose, fell to the ground, and bounced along the driveway.

"Oh!" exclaimed Claire. "That's not an *Activator* button, but a *Self-Destruct* button, which seems to be working quite well without even pushing it!"

Thomas glared at Claire. "Just give it to me before you wreck something else!" he snarled.

Claire hadn't noticed her hand slowly lowering while Thomas scrambled around her, but he did and with a desperate lunge he jumped up and latched onto his machine. One of the eggbeaters broke off in his hand. Claire still held the Transporter.

"Give it to me! Now!" he shouted.

Claire was enjoying the whole skirmish. "What are you going to do? Shoot me with a laser beam from that eggbeater you're holding?"

"It's not an eggbeater. It's an FRM!"

"An FRM?"

"A Frequency Reception Modulator! And now it probably won't work because you busted it!"

"Wow! A Transporter with a Frequency Receptor Modu-thingy. I didn't know they came with that feature. What will they think of next?"

"It's called a Frequency *Reception Modulator*. Now give me back my Transporter!"

Claire yawned. She was about to give the Transporter back when Thomas yelled, "I'm glad I let the air out of your bike tires! You're awful!"

Claire's eyes grew large and her jaw dropped. "You did what?!" she gasped.

She gritted her teeth and brought her arm back to throw the Transporter as far as she could. Thomas dropped the eggbeater and quick as a flash jumped up to hold Claire's wrist with both hands. Then he grabbed the Transporter, and as he did his hand hit the Activator.

Instantly, everything around them faded like the lights in a movie theatre just before the movie starts. They heard the faint, high-pitched sound of a distant siren. They started a kind of head-over-heels, slow-motion somersault as air quietly rushed past them.

This seemed to go on for a long time. Both Thomas and Claire felt dizzy. They began to feel warm. Then hot. The air became smoky. They could hear the roar of an engine. An enormous engine.

Then, with unexpected suddenness, they landed with a thud, face down on something hard.

Thomas yelped. He lay on his stomach, gripping a piece of dirty pipe. Claire was also on her stomach, behind Thomas, holding onto his ankles with all her might and screaming constantly.

They were on very hot metal which shook and jerked from side to side. They wanted to cover their ears because of the deafening roar in front of them, like the sound of an engine without a muffler, but they didn't want to let go of whatever it was they hung on to.

Black smoke blew in their faces and stung their eyes. The air smelled like burning tires.

Claire felt her long hair blowing around and whipping against her face. "What's happening?" she screamed above the noise. "Where... are we?!"

Thomas didn't answer. He gripped the piece of pipe harder. "I don't know!"

Discussion Questions

If you saw the Transporter, what would you think it was and why?

In what ways are Thomas and Claire typical kids?

Do you think siblings treat each other differently than they do other people? Why or why not?

At the end of the chapter, Thomas and Claire were transported to a new location. Where do you think they are now?

chapter 2

It took Thomas and Claire a while to figure out where they were. They couldn't believe how one minute they were on their driveway and the next they were lying on top of a train engine roaring down the tracks, black smoke spewing into their faces.

Claire screamed again, a loud and terrifying scream, but two long ear-piercing blasts from the train whistle drowned her out.

Thomas peered through the thick smoke coming from the stack in front of him and noticed small buildings in the distance. Before he could say anything, the train whistle blew two more long blasts. Claire wanted to cover her ears.

The train began to slow down, and as it did Thomas looked behind him and saw a line of train cars with scores of people sitting here and there on their roofs.

"We're not alone up here," he shouted to Claire. "Take a look behind you!"

Claire carefully turned her head, but not too far, afraid she might fall off. She saw a dozen men on the roof of the train car right behind them.

"They... they look like..." she stuttered, looking

at their clothes and skin colour. "What's going on, Thomas?!"

"I don't know," he yelled back. He swallowed, but his mouth was dry.

Claire closed her eyes and coughed. The constant plume of black smoke made her feel sick.

"Am I having some kind of weird dream?" she exclaimed after a few moments. "How can we possibly be here? We were just in our driveway! Now it looks like we're in India! What's going on?"

Thomas thought the people atop the train were more likely from Pakistan, but wasn't about to argue as he had other things on his mind—the piece of pipe he hung to suddenly broke off in his hands. The one screw holding it in place had fallen out. He was thankful the train was slowing; the sideways rocking motion also slowed. In a few minutes, the train came to a stop in a billow of black smoke.

An immense crowd of people surrounded the train, some meeting passengers, some getting off the train, some getting on. Goats mingled with the crowd and some people carried duffle bags or small crates. Claire saw a man with a basket of chickens on his head. The chickens were squawking as if a fox was in with them.

Claire got to her knees. "I'm scared! Let's get off this thing. I don't like it up here."

Thomas studied the people on the train platform—every person was brown-skinned. Some men and boys wore hats, without brims, sitting to one side of their heads. Most had long pants and tunics. Others wore long-sleeved white shirts. The women and girls were clothed in colourful dresses with long pieces of matching fabric wrapped around their waists and draped over their shoulders. Thomas noticed that many had red, powdery dots on their foreheads.

The noise of people talking, along with diesel trucks and buses coming and going, was almost as loud as the train had been.

Thomas sized it all up. "Okay. Let's get off. But… let's stick together."

That's when they noticed they wore the same clothes as the people on the platform. Thomas even had a brimless hat sloped to one side of his head.

"This is weirder than that neighbourhood costume party last autumn," he said.

"At least you're wearing some kind of pants," moaned Claire. "I've got this long dress thing on and these sandals aren't going to make it easy getting off here."

"You have sandals?"

Claire was closest to a ladder attached to the side of the engine. She started to climb down when she noticed the Transporter lying beside the piece of broken pipe.

"Thomas! The Transporter! Let's go back home!"

"Oh yeah!" he exclaimed, picking it up. "You know, I never actually expected it to do anything! I don't know how we got here. I don't know how it happened!"

Claire opened her mouth for a moment. "I'm as surprised as you are." She shivered. Tears came to her eyes. "Thomas, I'm totally freaked out!"

Thomas stared at the Transporter, then at the teeming crowd of people. "Claire, I'm going to push the Activator."

"W–wait," she stammered. "What if I don't go with you? If I'm not touching you, will I still leave at the same time?"

Thomas blinked a couple of times.

"I'd better touch you," said Claire. "I'd hate for you to leave without me."

"Right."

Thomas waited for Claire's hand to touch his foot,

then pushed the Activator. Nothing happened. He pushed it again, then shook the Transporter a couple of times. He tried the Activator again.

"I don't know why it's not working," he fumed.

"Is it because those parts fell off on the driveway?" asked Claire. "You know, the eggbeater and that other stuff?"

"The sparkplug and speaker magnet were just for looks," admitted Thomas.

"What about the eggbeater? You know, the Frequency Recirculating thing? Wasn't it just for looks, too?"

"Frequency Reception Modulator," corrected Thomas, his brow furrowed. "I don't know. This one FRM got us here somehow. Who knows what would have happened if it still had two FRMs." He scratched the side of his head. "I guess we'll have to go down. Maybe it'll work later."

They carefully climbed down the rickety steel ladder. When they got to the ground, they discovered they both had a cloth bag with a long strap hanging over their shoulders.

"What in the world is this thing?" wondered Thomas, noting the woven colours of his bag.

"I think it's a *jhola*," answered Claire.

"Yeah right! You're just making that up."

"No, I'm not! Ranjit at school uses one to carry his books. It's just like this one." Claire held up her *jhola*, then slid the strap off her shoulder, lifted the flap, and reached inside. "Hey, Thomas, there's some money in here!" She pulled out a large bill and held it for Thomas to see. "Fifty rupees."

"How much is fifty rupees?" asked Thomas. "Are we rich?"

"How should I know? Wait! There's also a can opener."

"A can opener? A can opener!" Thomas laughed. "Well, that'll sure come in handy."

"What's in your *jhola*?" inquired Claire.

Thomas fumbled with the flap covering the opening, then peered inside.

"Well, what's in there?" Claire demanded.

"I'm not sure."

"What do you mean, you're not sure? What is it?"

"It looks like four, I don't know, pears or something." He pulled one out for Claire to see.

"That's a mango," explained Claire.

"A mango?" Thomas held it in front of him and scrunched up his nose. "What's a mango?"

"It's like a pear."

"Oh, thank you," said Thomas. "You're so helpful."

The air on the platform was hot and smelled like spices and animals. Thomas and Claire stood there, wondering what to do, when a policeman in a blue uniform and white hat came along shouting orders. They didn't understand what he said but could tell by his hand motions that he wanted people to clear the area.

Thomas stuffed the Transporter into his *jhola*. It just fit. They walked along, squeezed and jostled by the enormous crowd. It was like being trapped in a slow-moving pinball game.

"Can you see where we're going?" Thomas called out, unable to see over the heads of the people.

Claire scanned the area. "We're moving toward some buses. People are getting on them. Thomas, what should we do?"

Thomas shrugged and glanced at Claire. "Hey, don't get so far away!"

The crowd had almost pushed Claire out of sight. In a moment, she would have been completely separated from

Thomas had not a huge Brahma bull wandered into the throng and forced them to go around it, pushing Claire back toward Thomas.

When they were together again, Thomas clutched Claire's arm. "I remember reading somewhere that cows are sacred in India."

"So, you agree we're in India?" asked Claire.

"Yeah, I guess so. It seems that way. But why?"

"Thomas, how should I know? Maybe we're still back home on the driveway and the Transporter knocked us out or something."

"No, we're here alright."

The noise of idling bus engines became louder.

Claire took Thomas' hand firmly in hers and peered over the mob. She saw an open space by the busses. "Let's go over to that red bus and try pushing the Actuator button thingy in your *jhola*."

"Okay," said Thomas. "By the way, that button thingy is called an *Activator* and…" He reached to pat the *jhola* slung over his shoulder, but it wasn't there. "Claire! My bag—it's gone!"

Claire stared at him in disbelief. Just then, she turned and saw a short man in a dirty brown sweater and ragged pants pushing his way through the crowd, holding Thomas' *jhola* above his head.

"Stop! Thief! Stop!" she yelled.

No one stopped the man, but he turned around long enough to see if he might get caught.

"Someone stop him!" screamed Claire. "Stop that man!"

There were hundreds of men in the crowd, but it was quite clear who Claire meant as she gestured wildly toward the scurrying thief.

Thomas crouched down and wove his way through the crowd like a snake in tall grass. He dove under a tall, hairy goat and up onto a cart that resembled an oversized wheelbarrow. From the edge of the cart, Thomas leapt. He landed perfectly—on a man next to the thief. Thomas reached out and grabbed the *jhola* from the thief, who let go and disappeared into the crowd.

Thomas reached into the *jhola* and brought out a mango, apologizing to the man he had landed on.

"Here," he said, handing him the mango. "Sorry for landing on you."

The man had a puzzled look on his face, but took the mango and walked away.

Thomas could feel his heart thumping in his chest.

Claire caught up to him, relieved to see he had the *jhola* back. "Are you alright?" she gasped.

"Yeah. I don't know how that guy slipped this jewela thing off my shoulder without me even noticing."

"It's called a *jhola*. Put the strap over your head so you don't lose it again. Now, let's get over to that red bus," she directed, squeezing Thomas' hand.

When they reached the bus, they stood by the front bumper, away from everyone. Thomas opened his *jhola*. When Claire had her hand on his shoulder, he pushed the Activator. Again, nothing happened. They stared at each other for a moment.

"The Frequency Reception Modulator is only at half power," Thomas scowled, "because you busted it."

Claire scrunched up her eyebrows. "Thomas… it's only an eggbeater!"

"But it got us here, didn't it?"

"You said you didn't know how we got here! How could an eggbeater possibly…" Her voice trailed off as she frowned at a row of idling diesel busses. "Thomas, I don't know how we got here, but if your Transporter did it with only one eggbeater… I mean…" She paused, searching for the right words. "If your Transporter got us here with only one Frequency Moderation Receptor, how come it isn't working now?"

"I don't know," mumbled Thomas.

Neither spoke for a few moments. A cow mooed somewhere.

"So now what do we do?" Claire asked as she surveyed the landscape of people. Her eyes widened. "I know! Let's phone home! Mom will know what to do."

They both scanned the area for a telephone booth.

"There aren't any power lines around here, let alone phone lines," Thomas said. "I think we're out of luck."

"What about using someone's cell phone? Cell phones are almost everywhere in the world."

"Sure. You find someone who has a cell phone, speaks English, and is willing for you to make a call from India to our house... and I'll buy you a root beer, which likely doesn't exist around here, either."

Claire sniffed as she wiped a tear from the corner of her eye. "Thomas, what are we going to do?"

He scratched his cheek. "Let's... let's get on this bus," he decided, pointing behind him with his thumb.

"Why should we do that?"

Thomas thought for a moment. "Maybe... Maybe we need to go somewhere higher. Maybe the Transporter only works at higher elevations. India is mostly at a lower elevation than where we live back home, but it's higher in the northern part of India. Maybe this bus is heading north."

"How come you know so much about India?"

"Hey, I pay attention in school, too, you know. You're not the only one who knows stuff."

"But what if this bus isn't heading north?" asked Claire. "What then?"

"Well, we'll figure it out," Thomas exclaimed. "Or maybe you have a better idea?"

Sometimes Claire just didn't understand her brother. If he were blindfolded and dropped into a strange city, he would thrive on the adventure of figuring out where he was and what he was going to do. As long as he didn't have to get dressed up for anything, like he had at their cousin's wedding last June, he was open to anything that might happen.

Claire, on the other hand, liked clear instructions and good plans, which was why she accomplished so much. She was comfortable with new situations, but only as long as she knew what was going on. The thought of boarding a bus bound for who-knows-where completely paralyzed her.

Claire's shoulders sagged. Not having any other ideas, she opened her *jhola*.

"I'll buy some tickets," she said with a sigh, handing the man at the bus door the fifty-rupee bill while pointing to herself and Thomas. The man gave her two tickets and ten rupees back.

Thomas spoke slowly to the ticketman and gestured with his hands. "Can you tell me where this bus is going?"

The man said something Thomas couldn't understand.

"Where's that?" asked Thomas.

The man shook his head from side to side.

"I feel much better now," moaned Claire as she got on the bus. "This is worse than driving with Granny. We have *no* idea where we're going!"

"At least with Granny we get to eat something. I'm hungry," Thomas groaned.

"You're always hungry. Why don't you eat a mango?"

"Very funny."

They found a seat near the back of the bus; they had to share the seat, since the bus was already jammed with people. In fact, there were so many people on the bus that sometimes two or three passengers had to share a seat. In a few minutes, even the aisle was crammed.

The man next to Thomas held a baby goat on his lap. Thomas hadn't noticed the goat until its wet nose nuzzled into his neck and its scratchy tongue took a lick. Thomas wanted to jump out of his seat, but there was nowhere to go. The goat gazed at him with curious, slit-like pupils. He found them quite intriguing, but then gently pushed the goat away. Its breath smelled like rotten onions. A lady behind him held two chickens and a man in front had a small monkey on a leash. Thomas felt like he was in some kind of mobile zoo.

The bus lurched as it pulled away from the train station and bounced along a bumpy road. Every so often it stopped and picked up more passengers until it was so packed with people and animals that Claire felt claustrophobic. An old lady squished beside her, put her head on Claire's lap, and fell asleep. Claire felt like she was in a bad TV movie that she couldn't turn off.

After almost two hours of bumping, jostling, and picking up and dropping off passengers, the bus turned into a village and parked in the main square. Thomas' ears were ringing by the time the engine stopped. Everyone got off.

Thomas and Claire took deep breaths of the fresh air. It smelled like pine trees. They found themselves in a market with tables of vegetables and oranges, raw meat, clothing, baskets, bottled water, goats in pens, and chickens in wicker basket cages. A cow wandered around helping itself to whatever it wanted to eat.

Claire began to walk around the market.

"What are you looking for?" asked Thomas, trotting along behind her.

"A hairbrush. Do you see any for sale?"

"No, I don't," answered Thomas, watching the cow eat a cauliflower from a table of produce.

He spotted a soldier standing near a table piled with woollen blankets and walked over to him.

"Can you tell me where this bus is going?" Thomas asked, pointing to the bus.

The soldier shrugged. "No speak English."

A lanky boy with jet black hair stood behind the blanket table. "I can talk English," he said. "This bus goes Barabeesay."

"What did you say?" asked Thomas, trying to understand his accent.

"This bus goes Barabeesay," repeated the boy, gesturing behind him to the mountains.

"Good. Really good. Uh... how far is Barabeesay?"

"Oh... thirty-five keelo-meters." He pointed again to the mountains, then added, "Maybe... three or four hours."

"Three or four hours? To go thirty-five kilometers?" Thomas scratched his head. "Why so slow? I could almost walk faster!"

The boy glanced toward the mountains. "The road is..." He motioned with his hand, starting down by his waist and angling up until it was higher than his head. "It is... step... no... steep." His hand flapped back and forth slowly like a flag in a light breeze. "And windy, very windy. And sometimes..." He swallowed and stopped talking.

"Do you mean that the wind blows a lot or that the road twists and turns?" asked Thomas.

"Yes! You are right, my friend!" exclaimed the boy. "Lots of turning! Lots of turning! And it is colder there. You should buy a blanket at this very moment, while you have the opportunity."

Thomas rubbed his chin. "How much for a blanket?"

"One hundred rupees."

19

Claire caught up to Thomas and overheard part of the conversation.

"Thomas," she whispered in his ear. "We only have ten rupees left!"

Thomas' eyes narrowed. He took a mango out of his *jhola* and looked straight at the boy. "How about ten rupees and a mango?"

The boy laughed.

"Ten rupees and two mangoes?" Seeing no interest, Thomas blurted, "Ten rupees and three mangoes! That's my final offer."

"I don't need mango," explained the boy, "but give ninety rupees and you can have beautiful warm blanket."

He unfolded a blanket and held it up, admiring it as he did so. Then he wrapped it around himself, gave a soothing sigh, and let his shoulders sag.

Claire scrunched up her nose. "How about three blankets for this can opener?" she offered, pulling the can opener out of her *jhola*. She held it in both hands, drawing as much attention to it as she could. The chrome handle flashed in the sun.

The boy looked away as the bus engine started.

The can opener handle opened in Claire's hands and she noticed some hidden parts.

"Oh! It has a bottle opener, a knife and... a tiny saw," she explained as she discovered what was in the handle. "And a small pair of pliers, and... a pair of scissors. Even a screwdriver!"

The boy's eyes widened. "Two blankets," he stammered. "I will give two blankets."

The bus engine revved a couple of times and people began to get on.

"Okay," accepted Claire, happy to get what she had intended all along. She handed the boy the can opener, took the blankets, gave one to Thomas, and walked toward the bus.

Thomas gaped at Claire, then at the hand-woven blanket in his hands. Wondering what had just happened, he caught up to her. "How'd you do that?"

"How'd I do what?"

"Get two blankets for that stupid can opener!"

"Remember what Grandpa used to tell us about buying and selling stuff?"

"No."

"Well, he said if you negotiate for more than you want, you might get what you were actually hoping for."

"Ohhhh." Thomas nodded, not exactly sure he understood what Claire had just said.

Before they reached the bus, they realized it was already packed full. Some people were sitting on the roof, so Thomas motioned for Claire to follow him around to the back of the bus. There, they found a ladder which they climbed. Thomas counted twenty-four people on the roof.

They clambered past a man with a basket full of chickens. The lid on top of the basket was crooked and Thomas wanted to straighten it out, but there were people in the way.

They sat down and faced each other, putting their backs against the low railing of the luggage rack. In a few moments, the bus started to move, vibrating and rattling as it did.

Within half an hour, the air became cooler. Thomas and Claire unfolded their new blankets and wrapped them around their shoulders.

The road became narrow, with many twists and turns and switchbacks. At one point, Thomas saw a steep drop into a deep gorge. A few minutes after that they came across another gorge, then another.

Claire moved closer to Thomas. "Try the Transporter again. This road has no guard rails, not even along the bridges! I'm... I'm not liking this bus ride." She looked around, her gaze stopping as she saw what was coming. "It would be nice to go home before we reach that pass up ahead."

"Who says we'll be going home?" asked Thomas.

"What do you mean?"

"Well, we might end up somewhere else first."

"Like where?"

"I don't know!"

"Well, you built it, didn't you?"

"Yes, but I didn't program it or anything, you know, to go to any particular place." Thomas put on a sweet smile. "Ladies and gentlemen," he said in a high-pitched voice, "please fasten your seatbelts and prepare to go to a tropical resort of your choice..."

"Very funny," said Claire. "You probably don't even know where in the world tropical resorts are."

"Why wouldn't I? I know where India is, don't I? Why wouldn't I know where tropical resorts are?"

"Okay," said Claire. "Where would you find a tropical resort?"

Thomas looked away. "I'm not telling you."

Just then, a bus coming from the opposite direction tore around a corner so fast that Claire thought both busses would crash. The side-view mirrors almost touched as the bus they were on jammed on the brakes.

"What happened?" shrieked Claire. "Did we hit them?"

Thomas peered over the side of the bus. "No," he replied calmly, watching half a dozen people climb off the roof. "The lid came off that chicken basket and some chickens flew out."

People ran in circles, trying to catch the chickens and pass them up to the roof of the bus, where they were stuffed back in the basket. The man who owned the chickens bowed in thanks to those who helped rescue them, then tied some string around the lid to keep it secure.

The bus started up again, rattling and shaking as it slogged along the bumpy road. It climbed high along the side of a steep hill, inching toward the pass ahead. The driver changed gears constantly as his ancient machine strained to keep moving.

Thomas pulled the Transporter out of his backpack. "Hold onto my arm," he said. "I'm going to push the Activator."

Claire put her hand on Thomas' arm. "How did you ever come up with such a ridiculous name for that button?"

"It's not ridiculous! I can call it what I want, can't I?"

"Then why not call it something... scientific?"

"Well, I was going to call it a *Foo-Foo* switch."

"A Foo-Foo switch?"

"Yeah. It's French or Spanish, or something, for fire."

"Wherever did you learn that?"

"Big Larry told me at school."

"How would he know? He doesn't speak French or Spanish!"

"No, but his aunt went to Europe last summer. I think it was Europe. Anyway, I think she told him."

"So... why didn't you call it a Foo-Foo switch?"

Thomas was quiet, then exhaled through his nose. "It just didn't sound very scientific."

The bus crested the top of the pass and Claire took a good look around. Her eyebrows lifted as she focused on the steep drop of the road ahead. About a kilometer away, the road disappeared around a corner. She shook Thomas' shoulder.

"Hurry up and push that button," she pleaded.

"Just a minute," said Thomas, noticing his untied shoelace. "Stuff your blanket into your bag. We might need it later." He did up his shoelace, stuffed his own blanket into his *jhola*, then secured the strap over his shoulder.

The bus began to pick up speed. The driver kept it in low gear to keep from going too fast, but this caused the engine to rev loudly. The revving engine reminded Claire of the train she and Thomas had been on not long before.

Just when it seemed like the engine might explode, there was a jolting, grinding sound and a loud bang. The revving stopped and the bus began to coast down the steep incline, picking up speed rapidly. Immediately, two men jumped off the roof. Five or six followed them, landing wildly on the road.

"Thomas!" yelled Claire, grabbing his sleeve. "We've got to get off. We're going to crash!"

The bus careened violently, desperate to stay on the winding road. Thomas heard the grating, screeching sound of brakes that weren't doing much. Squealing around one corner, he thought the wheels on one side of the bus might have actually come right off the road. He pushed the Activator constantly, but to no avail.

"It's not working!" he shouted.

"Keep trying! Keep trying!"

Thomas gave the Transporter a whack on the side of his leg as the bus headed into a particularly tight turn.

"We're not going to make it!" yelled Claire.

"Hang on!" Thomas shouted as he tried the Activator again.

Thomas and Claire found themselves flying through the air, a faint, high-pitched siren sound filling their ears. They were somersaulting, head over heels, as the air quietly rushed past them.

Thomas wondered if the bus had gone off the road, but the somersaulting went on for a long time. He figured if it had crashed he would have landed already.

The air began to smell like hot dogs and coffee. They could hear noise from a loudspeaker. Someone was talking very fast.

With a thud, they landed on a wooden bench.

They were in a room with a hundred or more people all sitting on benches and plastic patio chairs.

Thomas and Claire must have made some noise when they landed as several people nearby said, "Shhhhh!"

Suddenly, a man at the front of the room yelled *"Sold!"* as he pointed to a lady in an orange winter jacket. She walked to the front of the room and picked up a bedside lamp and box of canning jars.

Discussion Questions

What stood out for you about this chapter?

What made the bus ride unique?

Contrast Thomas and Claire before they leave home (Chapter 1) with how they relate to each other in India. Why do you think they treat each other differently?

At the end of the chapter, Thomas and Claire were transported to a new location. Where do you think they are now?

Thomas

Claire

chapter 3

Claire looked around at the assortment of people who filled the room. Many wore cowboy hats. Some had baseball hats. At the front of the room, a man stood on a platform and spoke into a handheld microphone. She didn't understand a word he said as he pointed to people who put up their hands. Also at the front of the room was some furniture: a green loveseat, a television in a maple cabinet, an oval coffee table, and several boxes.

"Thomas," Claire whispered, her heart still beating fast, "what do you think happened to the bus?"

Thomas shook his head but didn't say anything.

"Thomas?" Claire whispered again. "Where are we?"

He peered toward the back of the room and tried to figure out what was going on. Besides people seated on chairs and benches, a crowd stood along the back wall. He saw a sign that said "Hot Dogs and Coffee."

"I... don't know. I don't know," he repeated. "I do know one thing. This ain't no tropical resort." He scratched his armpit. "Hey, you're wearing jeans and a plaid shirt... and shoes! What happened to your India stuff?"

Claire looked at herself, then at Thomas. "It's the same for you. Except you have a baseball hat with a picture of a tractor on the front."

Thomas took off the hat and studied the picture. "That's a skid-steer," he corrected.

"Now who'll give me three dollars and go? Three dollars anywhere? Alright two dollars," called the man at the front of the room.

He spoke so rapidly that Thomas and Claire thought it sounded like another language. He held up a garden rake and looked over the crowd. He wore a grey cowboy hat, blue jeans, and a faded jean jacket. His cowboy boots were covered in mud. The paint on the concrete floor was peeling and some of the ceiling tiles had telltale stains of a leaking roof some time ago.

Several people put up their hands to bid on the rake. The man at the front of the room pointed to one of them. *"I'm bid now two dollars. Two-and-a-half anywhere?"* Three or four hands went up. The man's voice rose and fell like a musical wave. *"Alright, I'm bid two-and-an-half now, who'll give me three?"* He pointed to someone off to one side. *"Three dollars bid now, who'll give me three-fifty? Three-fifty anywhere?"* He scanned the room. *"Sold for three dollars!"* he called into the microphone, pointing to a man wearing a dirty baseball hat.

"That auctioneer is pretty good," whispered Claire to Thomas.

"How do you know that's what he's called? Oh right, you read about it somewhere," Thomas said, answering his own question before Claire could.

"No I never. But do you remember when Uncle Shane and Aunty Jenny told us about the auction they went to last summer? Remember, they bought that blue sofa for fifteen dollars then found all those coins inside it when they got home?"

Thomas nodded, eyeing the auctioneer and his large cowboy hat. "What's he saying? Do you understand what he's saying?"

"Sort of. He's trying to sell stuff to whoever will pay the most money."

"Yeah, but he's speaking so fast the words just seem to blend together."

Just then, two men on the platform brought up a massive red-brown wooden cupboard. *"Alright, what-am-I-bid?"* called the auctioneer. *"Who'll give me five hundred and go? Five hundred!"* The room was quiet. *"Four hundred? Four hundred anywhere?"*

Someone in the audience called out, "Three hundred!"

"Alright three hundred I'm bid. Who'll give me four? Three hundred now. Four anywhere? Four? Three-fifty?"

A few people raised their hands, and then things happened fast.

"Three-fifty bid now. Four hundred?" A woman wearing sunglasses put up her hand. The auctioneer pointed. *"Four hundred bid, four-fifty anywhere?"* Another hand went up. *"Four-fifty bid!"* called out the auctioneer, pointing to the man who'd raised his hand. Then he looked over at the woman who had bid four hundred and called, *"Five hundred?"* The woman gave a slight nod. The auctioneer looked back at the man. *"Six?"* A nod. Then he pointed to the woman. *"Seven?"* Another nod. The auctioneer pointed to the man. *"Eight?"* The man looked at the ground. *"Seven hundred dollars I'm bid, eight hundred anywhere, eight hundred?"* He surveyed the room. *"Seven- fifty?"* The crowd was hushed. The auctioneer paused. *"Sold! For seven hundred dollars!"*

Thomas looked at Claire. "Wow!" he exclaimed. "Three dollars for the rake and seven hundred for that cupboard."

A woman next to Thomas with dangly earrings and a hand-knit shawl over her shoulders spoke without moving her eyes from the front of the room. "I'd never pay seven hundred dollars for that thing," she said. "Last Saturday, one just like it sold for two hundred and twenty-five, and it came with a matching coffee table."

Claire stared at her for a moment, then leaned over and whispered in Thomas' ear. "Don't you wonder where we are?"

"We're at an auction."

"I know that much. But where?"

"Some place where most everyone is wearing a hat. I don't know. Just look for the Transporter. Mom's gonna wonder why we're so late for lunch." Thomas caught the smell of hot dogs, closed his eyes, and breathed deeply. He stretched his legs and put his hands in his pockets. He felt a piece of paper and took it out. It was a five-dollar bill.

"Hey, Claire! Look what was in my pocket!"

Thomas showed her the bill while he glanced over at the concession to see how much the hot dogs cost. They were two dollars and twenty-five cents.

"I've got five dollars, too!" exclaimed Claire as she pulled a bill out of her pocket. She craned her neck and saw a pay phone on the back wall. "I'm going to phone home. Wait here, and don't buy anything!"

She got up from her chair and walked to the back of the room.

The next item on the auction platform was a bedside table.

"Who'll give me a hundred dollars for this antique bedside table?" called the auctioneer into his microphone. *"Seventy-five? Fifty?"* No one put up their hands.

He went over to the bedside table and opened the door. The hinges broke and the door came off in his hands. A few people chuckled.

"Well maybe it ain't no antique, but if you fix it up, give it a coat o' paint, you'd have yourself a nice lookin'

bedside table." A grin spread across his face. *"Then... give it to your mother-in-law!"* More laughter. *"Ten bucks and go!"* he called out. No hands went up. The crowd was becoming disinterested.

"Okay, who's never been to an auction before and this is their first time?"

A dozen people in the crowd raised their hands.

The auctioneer called out as he pointed to each hand, *"Ten, twenty, thirty, forty, fifty..."* The crowd laughed. *"Alright,"* he smiled, *"who'll give me ten bucks and go?"*

Someone called out, "Five!"

"Alright five dollars I'm bid and who'll give me six?" A hand went up. *"Six bid and seven?"* Another hand. Eventually the bedside table with the broken hinges sold for twelve dollars.

Claire returned to her seat and slowly sat down.

"What's up?" asked Thomas. "What did Mom say? Is she worried about us? Is it still lunchtime?"

"The phone didn't work," answered Claire.

"What?"

"I got some change at the concession. When I phoned home, I got a message that our number was no longer in service."

"Maybe you dialled it wrong."

"No. I tried it three times."

"Maybe you should call collect or something."

"I did. Our number doesn't exist."

"Weird!"

Just then, one of the helpers on the platform put an apple box full of junk on the table beside the auctioneer. He reached in and held up some of the items inside—a vase, a frying pan, a few pairs of socks, and a blender. He dug around and then held up a jewellery box. He lifted the lid and put his microphone next to it. Musical chimes played "Silent Night." A few of the notes were off-key.

Thomas shivered involuntarily when he heard the sour notes.

"*Alright, here's a whole box full of valuable goodies including this nice little music box for the missus for Christmas time. Who'll give me five and go?*" He looked around the room and called into his microphone: "*Five dollars for the whole works.*" There was no response. "*Four? Three? Two dollars!*" A few hands went up.

The auctioneer began his musical banter. "*Alright now I'm bid now two dollars, two-fifty anywhere? Two-fifty?*"

Claire put up her hand.

The auctioneer pointed to her and said, "*Two-fifty I'm bid. Three anywhere? Three dollars?*"

Thomas turned to Claire, his eyes wide. "You're nuts! Why do you want that box of trash?"

"I don't want the trash. I want the music box."

"Why on earth would you buy that piece of junk? It can't even play 'Silent Night' in tune!"

"I collect music boxes. You know that. That one looks really old. Maybe it's an antique," answered Claire smugly.

"It's an antique piece of junk!" exclaimed Thomas.

"*Two-fifty bid, two-fifty. Am I bid three dollars, three anywhere?*"

A plump lady near the front put up her hand.

"*I'm bid now three dollars. Three-fifty anywhere?*" No one else put up their hand. Thomas questioned Claire with raised eyebrows.

Claire turned her head toward Thomas and said matter-of-factly, "It's not worth three-fifty to me."

Thomas was relieved. "Good thing!"

"*Alright now I'm bid three dollars, who'll give me three-fifty? Three twenty-five anywhere? Three dollars now...*"

Claire started to raise her hand.

"Don't do it!" commanded Thomas. "It's ridiculous for

us to buy anything. We have to get out of here! You don't want to lug that thing around. Besides, if you..."

Claire thrust her hand into the air. The auctioneer pointed to her and said *"Three twenty-five."* Then he looked at the plump lady. *"Three-twenty-five I'm bid now, three-fifty? Three-fifty?"* The lady hesitated, then nodded.

The auctioneer looked back at Claire. *"Hey now, three-seventy-five?"* Claire nodded. *"Three-seventy-five I'm bid, now four?"* The plump lady shook her head with a no-thanks look on her face.

"Who'll give me four?" He scanned the room to see if anyone else might be interested. *"Sold to the young lady!"* he called out, pointing to Claire. *"For three dollars and seventy-five cents."*

Thomas turned to Claire. "Now, that sure is interesting. It's not worth three-fifty, but it's worth three-seventy-five!" He sighed a deep sigh. "We might have needed that money for something, you know."

Claire ignored him as she scurried to the front of the room and picked up her box of treasures and the price slip.

Along one wall, near the platform, a lady sat at a table with a metal cashbox. After winning an auction, the buyer would go to the lady and pay for what they had bought. Claire gave her the price slip and three dollars and seventy-five cents. She had one dollar and twenty-five cents left in her pocket.

Claire returned to her seat and rummaged through her box. She was excited to find a hairbrush, but frowned when she saw it was full of hair. She put it back in the box. There was nothing else of any interest except an eggbeater in one corner, under several socks. Instantly, Thomas and Claire's eyes met. Thomas examined the eggbeater closely.

"Is it from the Transporter?" asked Claire.

"No. But it might work anyway."

"Thomas, do you think the Transporter is around here somewhere?"

"I don't know. It's bound to show up sometime, don't you think?"

"I hope so. I mean, this place is interesting and everything, but I would like to go home."

"I don't know why you just don't relax. You've got yourself a real nice music box," he teased, "that plays a unique version of 'Silent Night.' What more could you want?"

Claire frowned at him. She picked up the music box and pulled open a little drawer on the front. It was full of buttons.

"Alright, what do we have here?" called the auctioneer as his helper set a large stuffed animal on the platform beside him. It looked like it had been stored in someone's garage. The fur was dirty grey with tinges of faded yellow.

"Looks like a teddy bear that needs someone to love it."

A man in the crowd yelled, "Richard, I think you got yourself a raccoon, not a teddy bear."

The auctioneer placed the stuffed animal on the table beside him. The table was about a meter off the ground and the stuffed animal was almost a meter tall, so the auctioneer could look right in its eyes.

"Yep. We got us a raccoon here," he agreed, pointing to the black circles around the eyes. He reached behind and held up the striped tail. *"Yesiree. One fine raccoon. Alright, what am I bid? Who'll give me a dollar?"*

Five hands went up, which surprised the auctioneer.

"Must be a collector's item," he said. *"Worth a fortune I imagine. Alright now one dollar bid, who'll give me two? Two dollars for the collector raccoon!"*

Three or four people put up their hand, including Thomas.

"Thomas, what are you doing?!" questioned Claire. "What in the world are you going to do if you buy that thing? You can't take it with you!"

"Why not? If you can take your music box, why can't I take that raccoon?"

"You just told me we might need my money for something. And now you're going to spend yours!"

"Yeah. I might need your money to help me buy this raccoon!"

"Two dollars bid, who'll give me three? Three dollars? Two bid. Three? Three dollars anywhere?"

A man in a black cowboy hat at the back of the room put up his hand.

"Three dollars bid. Four. Four anywhere?"

"Thomas," pleaded Claire. "It's so ugly and worn out and... huge and..."

"I have space for it on my bed."

"With all the other stuffed animals on your bed, if you add that thing you'll have to sleep on the floor. It's ridiculous!"

The auctioneer looked like he would sell the raccoon to the man in the black cowboy hat when he said, *"Three-fifty? I'm bid now three dollars, three-fifty anywhere?"*

Thomas shot his hand into the air. Claire's jaw dropped.

The auctioneer pointed to Thomas. *"Three-fifty bid. Four dollars now? Three-fifty bid, four? Four dollars anywhere?"*

The man in the black cowboy hat put up his hand.

"Four bid now, four. Four-fifty anywhere? Four-fifty?"

Thomas put up his hand.

"Four-fifty now. Five? Five dollars?"

Thomas smiled at Claire. "Can I borrow the rest of your money?" he asked as sweetly as he could.

"Are you kidding? I would never forgive myself if you took that thing home. It's probably full of lice and... and fleas, and..."

The man with the black cowboy hat stared at his boots.

"*Sold! The collector raccoon to the young fella for four dollars and fifty cents.*"

Thomas had a grin like a Cheshire cat. He walked to the front of the room and picked up the raccoon. He could barely get his arms around it. He took it and the price slip, then paid four dollars and fifty cents at the pay table. He returned to his seat, still smiling.

Claire looked away at the far end of the platform and the lineup of household items to be sold. She closed her eyes and shook her head. When she opened them, her face went blank.

There, on top of a box full of pots and pans, was the Transporter. Claire poked Thomas in the ribs.

"Ow," he said. He frowned at Claire, then followed her gaze. When he saw the Transporter, he gasped. "The Transporter!" he almost shouted.

They stared at it for a few moments, then at each other, understanding what was about to happen.

"Maybe," began Claire, "maybe the money in our pockets was for us to buy the Transporter. Maybe we shouldn't have bought this stuff."

"What'll we do? What if we don't have enough money now?" asked Thomas. His eyes darted back and forth. "We'll have to sell something!" he blurted. "Here, let's sell the music box, and the rest of the junk it came with."

"What do you mean 'let's sell the music box?'" questioned Claire. "I want this music box." She opened the lid, but quickly closed it as the chimes began 'Silent Night.' "I know. Why don't we sell the raccoon? But I don't know who would want it. The man in the black cowboy hat is gone. He was the only other person willing to pay more than two dollars."

"This thing is worth a fortune!" exclaimed Thomas, admiring the raccoon. "People just don't know how valuable it is." On the platform, the box with the Transporter was moved beside the auctioneer. "We've got to hurry!"

The auctioneer held up a power saw and an electric drill. The drill's electrical cord had been cut and the power saw was missing the blade. When he put them on the table beside him, a piece of the power saw fell off and clanged on the floor.

"Alright, a couple of tools now for the home handyman. Maybe someone who's handy at fixing tools before he uses them!" A few people laughed.

"Allri…" The microphone started to cackle. *"Wh gi m… five d… and go? Fi doll… an g…"* The auctioneer's words were amplified in pieces.

"Richard, something's wrong with your mike!" someone shouted.

"Test, t… t…. est," the auctioneer called into his dying microphone. He lowered it to his side and called out in a loud voice, *"Folks, why don't you get yourself a hot dog and some coffee while we get another microphone up here. We'll just be a couple of minutes."*

"Now's our chance, Thomas!" exclaimed Claire. "Go and sell that raccoon!"

"I want to get a hot dog first. Let's see, I have fifty cents, and you have a dollar and twenty five cents, so that makes—"

"Thankfully not enough!" scolded Claire. "We might need every penny we have. Now, go sell that stuffed monstrosity!"

Thomas' eyes tightened. His bottom jaw jutted out. "I'll sell the raccoon, *if* there's someone with enough money. You go sell your pile of junk, including that music box," he added. "You'll be lucky if you get a buck for it!"

Claire studied the music box, her head tilted a bit to one side. She pulled out the little drawer to look once again at the collection of buttons inside. The drawer came right out and some buttons spilled on the floor. Thomas pushed his raccoon to the side and started to pick up the buttons. When he lifted his head he noticed something in the darkness of the missing drawer.

"Hey, what's this?" he asked, stopping Claire from putting the drawer back. He reached his fingers into the slot and pulled out a small gold necklace. On the necklace hung a tiny jewel. "Is that a diamond?"

"Looks like one, I think." Claire said, gently biting her bottom lip. "I'll sell the music box, but keep the necklace." She draped it around her neck.

"You think someone would actually buy a music box that's so out of tune? Good luck!"

"You want to sell that there music box?" came a voice from behind them.

Thomas and Claire turned around. The voice belonged to a lady wearing pink sweatpants, a baseball hat, and a green jacket that had a hockey-stick-shaped badge with the words "West Division" sewed on the sleeve.

The hat caught Thomas' eye. It looked like a pig's head with cloth ears sewed on each side, two black cloth eyes, and a cloth pig's nose for the visor. A curly wire tail stood up at the back. The lady's wispy grey hair flowed out from under the hat and her thick glasses made her eyes appear very large. The overall effect was quite unusual. Thomas stared at the hat until he realized Claire and the lady were talking.

"Yes, I do. What would you like to pay for it?" Claire asked.

"I'll give you five bucks."

"Six and it's yours."

"Six if you throw in the box of stuff it came with."

"I want to keep this eggbeater." Claire held it up for the lady to see. "And this," she added, lifting the jewel hanging from the necklace around her neck.

"Sure."

"Then it's sold for six dollars."

"Thank you," said the woman as she handed Claire the money and took the box.

Claire handed Thomas the eggbeater, which he put in his back pocket.

"Now it's your turn."

"My turn for what?"

"To sell the raccoon."

"Maybe we already have enough money to buy the Transporter," pleaded Thomas.

"And what if we don't?"

"Well, no one in this place has anywhere near enough money to buy this fella anyway," he said, stroking the raccoon's head.

"Well, why don't you sell it for what they do have?" suggested Claire. "And hurry. It looks like the auctioneer is getting ready to start again."

Thomas turned and saw the auctioneer walking across the platform with a different microphone in his hand. Thomas picked up the raccoon and raced to the back of the room.

I should be able to get twenty or thirty bucks easy for this guy, he thought. *Although I don't want to let it go for that little unless I absolutely have to.*

He was a little miffed when the first six people he asked to buy the raccoon said, "No thanks." One lady said, "Are you kidding?"

The auctioneer tested his microphone. *"Can you hear me alright at the back of the room?"*

Several people nodded. A stout, bearded man with a deep voice shouted, "Sure can, Richard. Loud and clear."

The auctioneer began to sell the electric drill and power saw.

Thomas changed his sales pitch, asking people if they'd like "a really good deal on a very expensive plush animal. A one-of-a-kind raccoon, a real collector's item."

No one was even slightly interested.

"Alright folks, let's get going on this here box of pots and other useful odds and ends." He reached in and held up the Transporter. *"Alright now. Here's an interesting contraption. Who'll give me ten dollars and go for this thing and all the other goodies in this here box? Ten dollars and go?"*

Thomas suddenly felt hot. He desperately tried to catch someone's eye. Anyone's eye. He saw a little old lady sitting in a chair at the back of the room, holding a small stuffed panda. He approached the woman and took a deep breath.

"You're probably in the market for a nice-looking raccoon to go along with that beautiful panda," he said hopefully.

The lady looked at the racoon as if she had just smelled something bad. For the first time, Thomas noticed it was missing an eye.

The lady pursed her lips. "Whatdya want fer it?" she asked, her gaze back on the auctioneer and what he was taking out of the box.

Thomas was about to answer when he noticed she had only three front teeth. He cleared his throat. "Uh, what would you, uh... what, um, do you think it's worth?"

"Oh, I dunno," yawned the lady as she scratched the side of her nose. "I wouldn't give you more than—"

"*Let's see what else is in here,*" called out the auctioneer.

He held a four-slice toaster in his hands. He set it beside the Transporter and then showed everyone an electric iron covered in black tar.

"*Ten and go for the whole box...*"

Thomas did a quick calculation in his head. *Claire has one dollar and twenty-five cents change. I have fifty cents, so that makes a dollar seventy-five. Claire got six dollars for the box of stuff. That's seven dollars and seventy-five cents...*

The lady focused back on Thomas. "Yeah, sorry. I don't think I'll..."

With the palm of his hand, Thomas quickly brushed the fur on the raccoon's head, what there was of it, trying to make it a little more attractive.

"Well," she said, "I'll give you two dollars, and not a penny more."

"*Alright, seven-fifty and go.*" Several hands shot into the air. The auctioneer began his musical chant. "*Seven-fifty bid, who'll give me eight?*" Four hands went up. "*Eight bid now, do I have nine? Nine dollars anywhere? Nine dollars? Do I have eight-fifty?*" A hand went up. "*Alright, nine anywhere? Eight-fifty bid. Nine?*"

"Okay," stammered Thomas.

Two dollars was better than nothing. He and Claire would then have nine dollars and seventy-five cents.

He put the raccoon beside the lady's chair. She opened her purse and took out a change pouch and began counting coins.

"*Alright, let's go with eight-seventy-five,*" called the auctioneer. The hand of a bald man eating a hot dog went up. So did that of a rather skinny man wearing a red toque. The auctioneer pointed to the bald man. "*And nine?*" The skinny man's hand went up. "*And nine-*

twenty-five?" The bald man's hand went up.

The lady handed some money to Thomas. "Here's thirty-five cents. And forty-five," she said, dropping another dime into his hand. "Oh, here's another quarter. That makes... uh... let's see..."

"Seventy cents," blurted Thomas. He could see the Frequency Reception Modulator on the Transporter.

"And here's another nickel. That makes seventy-five cents," counted the lady.

"And nine-fifty," called the auctioneer. *"Nine-fifty?"* The auctioneer needed to move on to other things. *"Nine-fifty going once, nine-fifty going twice..."* The skinny man's hand went up. *"Alright, I'm bid nine-fifty. Now nine-seventy-five?"*

Thomas glanced at the auctioneer.

"Nine seventy-five anywhere? Going once. Going twice..." The bald man looked away, then back again and put up his hand. *"Nine-seventy-five now bid. And ten?"* The skinny man looked out a nearby window.

"Ten dollars? Ten dollars anywhere?" the auctioneer pleaded with the skinny man, who shook his head. *"Nine-seventy-five bid, and ten? Ten dollars anywhere? And sol..."*

"Yeah!" called one of the auctioneer's helpers, pointing to Claire who had raised her hand. The late addition of another bidder surprised the auctioneer.

"Ten bid, and ten-twenty-five?" He looked at the bald man who shook his head. *"Ten-twenty-five anywhere? Anywhere?"* The auctioneer scanned the silent room. *"And sold over here for ten dollars,"* he called, pointing to Claire. She didn't go and get the box. She just sat there.

The lady buying the raccoon was still counting money. "And ten cents makes one-seventy-five. Oh, and here's another quarter, so that makes two dollars even."

"Thank you," said Thomas, feeling panicky. He knew the box with the Transporter had sold for ten dollars, but he didn't know to whom. He hurried back to Claire and sat down.

The auctioneer held up a well-used chainsaw. He tried to start it but couldn't get it going.

"Okay what am I bid for this gently-used chainsaw? Needs a new sparkplug probably, maybe it's outa gas..."

"Claire, I just got two dollars for the raccoon!" said Thomas proudly. "That means we have nine dollars and seventy-five cents altogether. Now we can buy the Transporter from whoever just bought that box of stuff!"

Claire slowly turned toward Thomas.

"You only got two dollars for the raccoon? You paid four-fifty and got two? Thomas, we needed more than two dollars!"

"Well, this isn't a crowd that appreciates value," explained Thomas. "Besides, whoever paid ten dollars for that box of junk will easily take nine dollars and seventy-five cents for the Transporter."

Claire gritted her teeth. "Thomas, *I* just bought that box of junk!"

Thomas' face went blank. "What? *You* bought it? But... but you paid ten dollars for it!"

"Don't I know that?"

"But we only have nine dollars and seventy-five cents!" stammered Thomas. Claire stared at the ceiling and exhaled.

Thomas wrung his hands. "Maybe we can sell some of the stuff in the box and make up the difference," he suggested.

"Thomas, we can't sell any stuff until we pay for it first."

"Good point," agreed Thomas. "I should have demanded more for the raccoon. I gave this lady a real deal."

Claire rolled her eyes.

"I've got an idea," blurted Thomas. "We'll go get the box, and on the way to the pay table we'll push the Activator and get out of here."

"No. That might be risky, Thomas. It's so crowded in here. What happens if someone is touching us when we do? They might go with us."

"Good point," agreed Thomas. "Well, then... we get the Transporter out of the box and run for the door and activate it outside where there aren't any people."

"What if it doesn't work?" Claire frowned. She thought for a moment, then realized she was fiddling with the necklace around her neck. She looked at it, then mournfully said, "Maybe I could sell this."

"Great idea!" exclaimed Thomas. "It might be worth twenty-five cents, if you're lucky."

Claire took off the necklace and eyed it longingly. She sighed as her shoulders dropped.

"Okay. I'll try and sell it. You get the box of stuff. I'll meet you at the pay table."

Thomas walked over to the platform where the auctioneer was selling a mannequin with one ear missing. Someone had drawn a handlebar moustache and thick arching eyebrows on the face with a felt marker.

"Looks like a relative of mine," said the auctioneer, *"except he isn't missing an ear."* A few people chuckled. *"He's missing both ears!"*

Thomas picked up the box Claire had bought, and the price slip with it, then walked slowly to the pay table, wanting to give Claire as much time as possible to sell her necklace. She got there before he did.

"Did you sell it already?" he asked.

"Yeah."

"That was fast. How much did you get?"

"I got two dollars and twenty-five cents," said Claire,

a grin on her face.

Thomas put the box on the floor and together they gave the cashier ten dollars. Thomas picked up the Transporter.

"Let's go outside," he said.

They walked out the doors to a grassy spot near a spruce tree. Other people were around, but no one close by.

"Who did you sell that necklace to?" asked Thomas.

"A little old lady," replied Claire. "It was funny because your raccoon was sitting right beside her."

"What?" gasped Thomas. "That's the same lady who... but it took her forever to pay me!"

"Well, she offered two dollars and twenty-five cents and paid me right away."

"How much do we have left over now?" Thomas scrunched up his eyes, then opened them wide. "We have two dollars, right? Right?"

"Yes. That's right."

"Great! Give it to me and I'll go buy the raccoon back, then we can—"

"Thomas!" Claire interrupted. "We're leaving. Now!"

Thomas looked up at his sister. She somehow seemed taller. "Uh... okay," he said resignedly. "But I'm gonna regret it. That raccoon was a real treasure. One of a kind."

Claire slowly shook her head in disbelief.

Thomas' eyes grew large again. "Hey! Let me at least go and buy a hot dog. I'll be real quick."

"And how much are they?" inquired Claire, already knowing the answer.

Thomas' shoulders sagged as he remembered. "Two-twenty-five," he moaned.

"Fix that eggbeater modulator thingy and then let's get going."

"Right." He took the eggbeater out of his back pocket and jammed it into the top of the Transporter. Claire put her hand on Thomas' shoulder as he pushed the Activator.

There was a high-pitched siren sound. The voice of the auctioneer began to fade, as did the smell of coffee and hot dogs. Thomas and Claire slowly spun head over heels, the air quietly blowing past their faces. As they somersaulted through the air, they began to hear the sound of rain.

The rain got louder. The air was cool. It was very dark.

Suddenly, Claire landed hard on an overgrown lawn and immediately felt the wet grass soak her clothes. She got up and shivered. Thomas landed on a pile of garbage bags beside a dumpster. The smell of stinking garbage made him jump to his feet.

"Claire?" he called. "Claire, where are you?"

Claire could hear Thomas but couldn't see him. "I'm over here!"

"Where's 'here'?" asked Thomas, trying to locate her voice over the sound of rain splattering on the garbage bags.

Discussion Questions

What problem did Thomas and Claire have after they bought the music box and raccoon?

Thomas and Claire felt that each other's purchases were stupid. Why?

Imagine there is something at the auction you really want. What would it be?

How could someone like Thomas or Claire convince you it wouldn't be a wise purchase?

At the end of the chapter, Thomas and Claire were transported to a new location. Where do you think they are now?

chapter 4

As Claire's eyes adjusted to the darkness, she saw Thomas standing with his back toward her. "Behind you, Thomas," she called out. "Here I am."

Thomas turned and walked quickly toward her. He didn't see a cat in his way and stepped on its tail. It let out a shrieking *meow*. Both Thomas and Claire jumped. Claire could feel her pulse beating.

"Thomas, I'm scared, let's get out of here. Mom and Dad are probably worried about us. Let's go home. Do you have the Transporter?"

"No. I don't know where it is. I don't know where *we* are. I'm cold. This is freaky."

"What should we do?" stammered Claire, gripping his arm.

"What are you wearing?"

"I can't tell. Some kind of jacket. But it's definitely not waterproof."

"Yeah, same. Anything in your pockets?"

"No."

"And no hat," Thomas added, wiping the rain running down his forehead with his sleeve. He slowly turned around. He could see the light of a streetlamp in the distance. He shivered.

"Let's walk toward that light and then figure out what to do," he suggested.

Claire felt the rain dripping down her neck. "Thomas," she whispered, "could we... hold hands?"

Normally Thomas would have laughed at such a question and mocked his sister. But not now. "Sure," he answered quickly.

They were in a lane with dark buildings on either side. Dim light shone through a broken window in a building some distance away. Through the window they could see a single bulb hanging from a wire.

"Let's go to that building and ask for help," he suggested.

As they approached the building, a dog behind the fence suddenly let out a deep, fast, angry bark. Even with the fence between them and the dog, Thomas and Claire jumped and ran off toward the streetlamp.

They couldn't see the deep puddles they stepped in and soon their shoes were soaked. Finally they were close enough to the streetlamp that some of its light actually lit up the lane.

Just then, three dark figures came around the corner and walked toward them. Thomas and Claire could see their silhouettes, but not their faces. They were three boys, the two outside boys taller than the middle one. They wore baseball hats with the visors turned backwards.

The middle boy wore a hoodie and spoke gruffly. "Hey! Where do you think you guys are goin'?" he asked Thomas and Claire, the streetlamp exposing their wide eyes.

Neither Thomas nor Claire said anything.

"Whatsa matter? Don't talk English?"

"Uh..." said Claire. "We... we were going to... uh... We're kinda lost."

"No kidding!" smirked one of the boys.

"Well," said the middle boy, "welcome to Rebel Warrior territory."

"Thank you," said Thomas. "Can you tell us how to get out of here?"

"What's your names?"

Thomas swallowed. "I'm Thomas and this is my sister Claire." No one else introduced themselves, so he asked, "What are your names?"

One of the boys chuckled.

"I'm Harley," said the middle boy. "This is Ace and Stoker." He gestured to the boys on either side of him.

"Well, nice to meet you," Thomas said, trying to make his quivering voice sound as confident as possible. "Now, if you wouldn't mind, you know, telling us—"

"How'd you get here?" interrupted Harley.

Thomas cleared his throat. "Well, I... I built a Transporter," he began, speaking rapidly, "and it takes us from place to place. Have you seen it? It looks like a block of wood with two eggbeaters attached to it. I'd really appreciate it if you..." Thomas noticed Harley staring at him. "If you... would..."

"You're nuts," announced Harley. He turned to Ace and Stoker. "Show these two visitors a warm Rebel Warrior welcome. The kind where they won't be traipsin' around here again."

Ace began to raise his right fist.

Claire grabbed Thomas by the arm, but before they could make a run for it a police car suddenly raced toward them from the far end of the lane, siren blaring and blue and red lights flashing. Harley, Ace, and Stoker turned to run the other way when another cruiser came barrelling around the corner behind them, blocking their path. In a moment, a spotlight from one of the cruisers shone on the group. Two police officers jumped out from each car and stood behind open doors, guns drawn and pointing at Harley.

"Alright, Harley!" commanded one of the officers. "We've got you now. Put your hands up and move over here slowly."

"What? What's this all about, man?" questioned Harley in disbelief. He slowly raised his hands, as did Ace, Stoker, Thomas, and Claire.

"Yeah right!" the officer said. "McKernan Grocery Store gets robbed two minutes ago and you don't know anything about it? Get in the cruiser!"

"I swear, man, it wasn't me!"

"Funny how the description matches you! Let's see you walk without a limp."

"Excuse me, officer," interrupted Thomas, not actually knowing if he addressed the policeman correctly. "We've been talking with Harley and his friends here for about five minutes before you came and they've been here the whole time."

"Thomas James!" exclaimed Claire in a forceful whisper.

"Is that so?" said one officer. "And who are you?"

"I'm Thomas Brampton and this is my sister Claire."

"Where do you live?"

"Well..." Thomas opened his mouth as he thought about what to say. "Well, we... we just kinda..."

"Car 19!" one of the cruiser radios crackled. "Robbery suspect located on Bannerman Avenue heading east. Backup requested!"

"Let's go!" shouted an officer. The policemen jumped in their cars. In a moment of revving engines and screeching tires, they were gone.

No one said anything. Claire heard raindrops in the puddles nearby. She wished she'd asked the police for help.

It was Stoker who spoke first, looking at Thomas. "Why'd you say that when a moment ago we were going to paste you guys?"

"It was true, wasn't it? You were here the whole time." Thomas turned to Harley. "Did you just rob the McKernan Grocery Store?"

"No," answered Harley. He put his hands in his pockets. "Not tonight."

Ace and Stoker chuckled.

"Besides," added Thomas, "you don't have a limp."

Harley turned and in the light of the streetlamp Claire saw a grin spread across his face.

"Hey, you're alright. You're okay," Harley said, nodding his head. He suddenly became serious. "Let's move." He signalled with his arm for everyone to follow him.

"Is this a good idea?" whispered Claire to Thomas.

Thomas followed Harley as they walked into the darkness. He turned to Claire. "What choice do we have?"

The group moved back down the lane the way Thomas and Claire had just come. Claire thought it seemed darker than before. Thomas felt uncomfortable between Harley in front and Ace and Stoker behind, but he remembered what he had just told Claire. What choice did they have?

He bent down to tie his shoelace. Claire stopped to wait for him, but Stoker growled, "Keep moving!"

After a few minutes of tripping over the uneven surface of the pavement and continually stepping in puddles, the group turned toward a fence and Harley opened a creaky gate. Without warning, a huge dog shattered the silence with angry barking. The dog's vicious snarls made Claire shiver.

"Shut up, Roxy!" Harley yelled. It slinked into a corner of the yard.

Thomas, distracted by the size of the dog, bumped into Claire, which made her scream. That's when she realized it was the same yard she and Thomas had thought about entering earlier. A glowing light bulb could be seen through one of the building's broken upper windows.

They walked past the growling dog to a side door. Harley opened the door and walked down some stairs. The air smelled damp and musty. He flicked his cigarette lighter and led the way along a narrow hallway. Claire almost banged her head on the low doorframe as they entered a black room. Using the light of the flickering flame, Harley twisted a lone bulb hanging from the ceiling.

The light revealed a round kitchen table and four wooden chairs. The dirty chairs were badly chipped, showing that they had been painted several times. The two windows in the room were covered with plywood. There were holes in the ceiling and someone had drawn all over the walls. The floor was littered with garbage and there was a pool of water in one corner.

In the bright light, Claire and Thomas could see Harley's face clearly. He had sunken eyes and a scar on his right cheek. His bottom lip was swollen. He pulled back his hoodie to reveal a mess of tangled brown hair and a ring in each ear.

"Have a seat," he offered Thomas and Claire.

Claire brushed some dirt off the seat of the chair closest to her and sat down. Thomas just sat down. One leg of his chair was missing a foot and the chair wobbled depending on which way he leaned. He leaned back and forth several times, trying to decide which lean was more comfortable. Stoker and Ace stood against the wall by the doorway.

"Stoker, get us some drinks," ordered Harley as he sat down.

Stoker left the room and in a moment returned with a

six pack of root beer. He put it on the table. It happened to be Thomas' favourite brand and he began to feel that things weren't so bad after all.

"So," said Harley as he handed out the cans, "you're Thomas and Claire." He opened his can and took a long drink. "Tell me something. Why aren't you guys afraid of us?"

"I am, sort of," admitted Claire, trying to lift the tab on top of her can.

"Why should we be?" Thomas asked, taking a long drink. He banged the can back on the table a little harder than he had expected. Harley stared at Thomas for a moment, trying to decide what Thomas might have meant by smacking the can so hard.

Before he could say anything, Claire spoke up. "Harley, where are your parents?"

Stoker and Ace both stopped drinking, then looked at Harley, who put his can on the table, got up slowly, and took two or three steps with his hands in his coat pockets. He stood still, then sat down again and cleared his throat.

"Don't know," he answered. He was quiet for a while. "I ran away from home two years ago. Haven't seen them since."

"Why did you run away from home?" inquired Claire softly.

Harley looked away, then suddenly and angrily growled, "Listen, it doesn't matter, alright? Everyone has troubles. I'm sure you've got yours. Like how you guys ended up in this part of town. We could have pounded you before the cops showed up, you know."

There was a long pause. Both Thomas and Claire thought about their mom and dad back home and the fact that they had a home and how they wanted to be there.

"If you could be anywhere else in the world, doing anything else, what would it be?" Claire asked.

Ace jumped into the conversation. "I'd be a Formula One race car driver. That'd be so cool. I'd travel all over Canada and the States. It'd be awesome."

Stoker glanced at Ace, then took a breath. "I'd go see my uncle and aunt in Kitchener. They have the coolest home. I always felt good there. I haven't been there for..." He looked away. "...a long time."

"Who cares?" snapped Harley. "We're the Rebel Warriors and this is our life, so let's just quit this stupid daydreaming! Who cares where we'd like to be or what else we'd like to be doing? This is where we are and this is where we'll stay!"

"Well," Claire objected, "why can't things change?"

"Oh, give me a break!" sneered Harley. He spat on the floor. "What do you know about anything? You don't have a clue what it's like here! We live where there's no hope. None! It's survival. If you don't grab what you can, someone else will grab what's yours." He took a drink and then banged the can hard on the table. "No time for dreaming!" He kicked the empty chair beside him and it crashed to the floor.

There was a long silence.

"My dad's an alcoholic," Ace mumbled, staring at a hole in the ceiling. "My mom left him. I don't know where she lives anymore."

"I know where my parents live," said Stoker, "but they don't care about me anyway and I don't care about them." He took a last gulp of root beer and threw the empty can into a dark corner. It bounced off the wall and hit what sounded like a pile of empty cans.

Claire placed her drink on the table. "Isn't there anywhere you could go, you know, to make a fresh start?"

"Yeah right!" snarled Harley. "Where? Where could we

possibly go?" He looked down at his feet and lowered his voice. "We have no options."

Thomas suddenly burped. It was one of those burps that startles everyone, including the person who burped. "S'cuse me," he said. "I was, uh... I was wondering if maybe there's some options you haven't thought of or heard about yet."

Harley opened his mouth to speak when Roxy started barking.

"Shut up!" someone yelled outside. There was a loud knock at the door.

Harley motioned to Stoker, who slipped into the dark hallway. In a moment he returned with an older boy who had black hair and a goatee. He wore sunglasses. Thomas wondered how this new guy could see anything when it was so dark outside. Then Thomas noticed the blood by his ear and the jagged rip in his coat.

"B.T.!" Harley gasped. "What's up? What happened to you?"

B.T. took off his sunglasses. He had a black eye and Thomas saw he was missing a front tooth. "Anjou's comin' this way," he said in a tone that both Thomas and Claire could tell meant trouble.

"No way!" Harley jumped to his feet. "I thought he skipped town!"

"He did," confirmed B.T. "But he's back and wants revenge."

"Where's he right now?" demanded Harley.

"I ran into him and his gang on Fifty-Third Street about half an hour ago. We had a bit of a scuffle. The cops showed up and they scattered. I barely got away myself." B.T. noticed Thomas and Claire. "Who are these dudes?"

"They're Thomas and Claire. They're okay," answered Harley. He glanced furtively around the room, then his eyes settled back on Thomas and Claire. "We need to get you guys out of here, then lay low at Gleddies 'til this thing cools down." He walked around the table, stopped in the hallway, and spoke fast. "Ace, you and B.T. fly over to Fifty-Third Street and if you see Anjou..." Harley zipped up his jacket and swallowed. "...distract him long enough for me and Stoker to get Thomas and Claire clear. Then head to Gleddies and wait for us. Don't get caught. If Anjou gets you, you don't know nothin'. Got it?"

The others nodded.

In a moment Stoker had unscrewed the light bulb and the group felt their way along the dark hallway to the stairs and out the door. The rain had stopped and the clouds had mostly cleared. A full moon lit the yard. Roxy cowered in the tall grass and growled as they walked by.

"Where are you going to take us?" asked Claire.

"To a bus stop so you can get out of here," explained Harley.

They walked briskly to the end of the lane and turned onto the street. Two blocks further, they stopped under a streetlamp.

Harley pointed down the road. "This is it. Go about four or five blocks east and you'll come to a bus stop. Good luck."

"You're going to need it," came a gruff voice behind them.

They turned to see a group of twelve boys emerging from the shadows. The voice had come from the leader.

"Anjou!" gasped Harley. "I thought... I... I thought you'd left town for better places."

"I did. But I had some unfinished business to attend to," Anjou snarled as he walked closer.

Thomas saw that Anjou was about the same height as Harley, with the same kind of hoodie.

"Who arc these two creeps you're holding hostage?" Anjou asked, gesturing to Thomas and Claire. "Friends of yours?"

"Yeah, that's right. Listen, they were just leaving."

"I'm sure they were," sneered Anjou, walking right up to Harley. "Maybe we could escort them—and you—somewhere that might help you remember who's boss around here."

The gang around him snickered and began to close in around Harley, Stoker, Thomas, and Claire. Each gang member rubbed one fist into the palm of their other hand.

Except for one boy. He was holding Thomas' Transporter. Stoker saw it first.

"Hey! That's the Transportal thing Thomas told us about," Stoker blurted, pointing to it.

"Who's Thomas and what in the world are you talking about?" demanded Anjou. He looked at the Transporter, then at Thomas. "You must be Thomas."

Anjou grabbed the Transporter from his sidekick and examined it closely. He tried pulling off one of the eggbeaters, but it wouldn't budge. He walked toward Thomas. That's when Thomas noticed Anjou had a limp.

"So... what's this thing worth to you?" asked Anjou.

Thomas' eyes widened. Suddenly, he had an idea.

"Hey, Anjou," Thomas said. "What if I told you I knew something about you that could get you into a lot of trouble?"

Anjou walked right up to Thomas and looked down in his face. "Like what? I've never seen you before in my life!" He pushed his clenched fist against Thomas' chin. "What could you possibly know about me, you little jerk!"

Thomas spoke quickly. "Well, I happen to know you robbed the McKernan Grocery Store tonight!"

Anjou's face went blank. Thomas was very much aware that he had everyone's attention, but he didn't know what to say next. This felt like the time he'd stood in front of his whole school to recite a poem and his mind went blank. He looked around at the group of scowling boys and felt desperate for a thought to come to him. Any thought. He could feel his heart pounding. His mouth was dry.

Then he noticed the flashing lights of police cars in the distance, coming toward them. Another idea popped into his head.

"Anjou, if you had half a brain, you'd give me that Transporter right this minute. Before the police show up."

Anjou couldn't believe what he had just heard. Neither could Harley. Anjou's gang pressed closer. Anjou gritted his teeth.

"And if you had the other half, you'd turn yourself in," Thomas continued.

Anjou looked like he hadn't understood a thing Thomas said. He raised his clenched fist.

Just then, they heard sirens.

"Cops!" someone yelled.

"Let's fly!" Anjou commanded, dropping the Transporter. He and his gang scattered in all directions.

Soon, only Thomas, Claire, Harley, and Stoker remained.

The police cars were still several blocks away, but coming quickly. Harley and Stoker began to run.

Harley stopped and turned around. "Hey! Thanks, Thomas and Claire," he said, grinning slowly. "Thank you."

Thomas waved. "Good luck, Harley!"

Claire stared at Harley. "I hope your dreams come true!"

Harley smiled, raised a thumb, then turned and ran after Stoker.

Thomas picked up the Transporter. "Let's go," he said to Claire.

She walked over to him, still watching Harley and Stoker as they disappeared into the night.

Thomas took a deep breath. "Wow, I can hardly believe what just happened!"

"Or what almost happened," Claire added, breathing rapidly. "Thomas, I really want to go home now!"

"That might happen. I guess. Maybe."

Claire put her hand on his shoulder as Thomas pushed the Activator.

They began the familiar slow motion head-over-heels somersault. The police sirens got louder and louder, then softer. The air rushed past them, quietly. This seemed to go on for a long time.

As Thomas and Claire spun through the air, they began to see where they would land: there were four padded chairs with dark wooden armrests, almost like thrones, covered in a heavy red velvet material. As the chairs came into view, both Thomas and Claire squirmed and twisted so they would land on the chairs in a sitting position.

Claire landed properly on one chair. Thomas misjudged his landing and caught his right leg on the armrest of another. He bounced forward and hit his head on the floor.

"Ow!" he cried out.

"Quiet! Please!" someone whispered loudly nearby. Claire turned and saw a tall lady in a long black gown standing by a dark wooden door. "The session is about to begin. You must be quiet. Thomas! Get off the floor immediately!"

Discussion Questions

Describe what it's like where Thomas and Claire find themselves and how they feel about it.

What do you know about Harley, Ace, and Stoker?

Why is it tempting to judge people like them?

If Harley, Ace, or Stoker asked you for advice about how to change their circumstances, what would you tell them?

At the end of the chapter, Thomas and Claire were transported to a new location. Where do you think they are now?

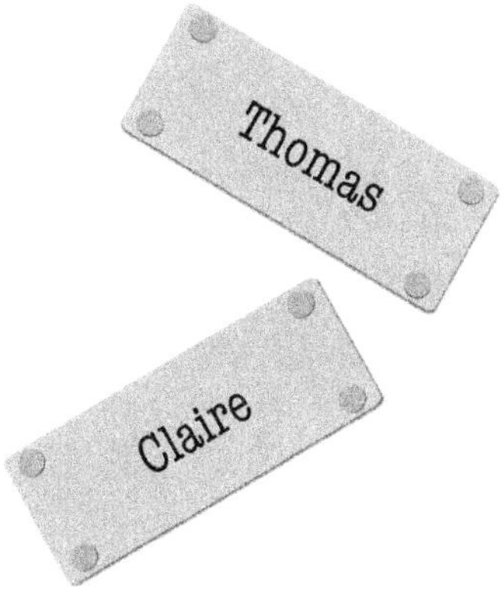
Thomas
Claire

The tall lady in the long black gown looked like a judge. She peered through the crack in the slightly open door in front of her, then turned to Thomas and Claire.

"It's almost time for you to go into the Chamber," she said. "Oh yes. Here is the Members map. Some of the Members have moved around a little since last session." She handed them each a piece of paper.

Thomas stood and rubbed his bottom where he'd landed on the armrest. "Where are we?" he started to whisper, but Claire held her finger to her lips.

She stared at Thomas. He wore dark blue slacks with a crease, a white shirt with a red tie, a blue dress jacket, and shiny black shoes. On the pocket of the jacket was a crest—a coat of arms with a small lion on one side and what looked like a deer on the other. Then she noticed he was staring at her. She wore the exact same clothes.

The tall lady held several file folders, two of which fell on the floor. Papers spilled all over. "This session will likely be very busy," she fumed as Thomas and Claire helped pick up the mess, "so please remember everything you've been told."

"Excuse me, ma'am?" asked Claire.

"Miss Phelps," corrected the lady.

"Miss Phelps, would you quickly highlight... some of the important things to remember... you know... quickly for us?"

"Certainly," said Miss Phelps, standing to her feet. "First, no talking in the Chamber. Be attentive to Members who have messages for you to deliver and remember to deliver the messages promptly. Remember, don't run in the Chamber, but walk quickly. Always move back to your positions by the railing when you have finished delivering a message."

Both Thomas and Claire nodded, trying to grasp what she was talking about.

Miss Phelps studied Thomas and Claire for a moment. "You're both new, aren't you? We don't normally have *two* new Pages at the same time," she exclaimed, pushing her glasses higher up on her nose, "but that's just the way it worked out today. It's not often the Legislature convenes on such short notice and at such a late hour. I'm just glad I could find four Pages at all!" She looked closely at Thomas. "You don't look like you're even old enough. Well, never mind. The session will be starting any moment now. We really should have six Pages, but four will have to do."

Thomas looked at Claire like he thought Miss Phelps was loony.

"Where are the other two Pages?" asked Claire, beginning to figure out what was going on. Apparently she and Thomas were called "Pages." Thomas, on the other hand, thought Miss Phelps was talking about pieces of paper.

"Don't you remember that from your training? They'll be going in and standing with you along the railing by the Speaker's chair. They'll line up with you, of course."

"Of course," said Claire. "They'll line up with us."

"Exactly," said Miss Phelps.

"Exactly," echoed Thomas with a pained expression on his face.

"And don't forget," added Miss Phelps. "Government MLAs are on the right side as you walk in, and the Opposition is on the left. I need to go now. When this door opens, it will be time to line up behind the Clerk Assistant. Remember the order: Sergeant-at-Arms, Speaker, Clerk, Clerk Assistant, and Pages. Got it?"

"Got it," chimed Thomas and Claire.

Miss Phelps took a breath, exhaled through her nose, then turned and marched down the hallway, her long gown sweeping the floor as she walked away.

"Thomas," whispered Claire, "I think we're in a legislative assembly somewhere!"

Thomas looked at her with one eyebrow raised. "Cool. What's a registration assembly?"

"*Legislative* assembly. It's a place where people in the government decide what should happen to everybody. You know, rules and laws and stuff like that."

"What's that got to do with us?" asked Thomas, fidgeting with his tie, trying to loosen it a little. "Listen, let's get out of here! I'm finding this tie a little tight and—"

"Thomas, do you have the Transporter?"

"Well... no."

"Then we might as well go along with what's happening until it shows up. Besides, this is kinda fun, don't you think?"

Thomas' head was cocked to one side, like his dog Bartholomew when opera played on the radio.

"No, I don't think this is kinda fun," he said. "I don't think this is kinda fun at all! I think this is kinda weird. We're wearing strange clothes and we're called Pages and I don't have a clue what Miss Phelps was talking about. I don't like it at all." Thomas looked around. "Since we don't have the Transporter, I say we hide somewhere until it shows up!"

"Thomas, just relax!" said Claire. "By the way, how's my hair?"

"Oh, brother!" Thomas exclaimed.

Just then, the dark wooden door opened wide.

"Come on, Thomas, let's go," directed Claire.

"But I have no idea what I'm supposed to do!"

"We're supposed to line up behind the Clerk Assistant."

"Oh, thank you. I feel better now," whined Thomas as he rolled his eyes. "What on earth is a Corked Assistant?"

"Not *what*," answered a voice behind him, "but *who*. And it's *Clerk* Assistant, if you please."

He turned to see a kind-faced gentleman who carried something that surprised Thomas. It looked like a long gold-covered wand imbedded with all kinds of jewels. On one end was a small crown. The man was dressed in a fancy blue jacket and a shirt with a high collar and white ruffled sleeves.

Thomas walked over to him. "What's that you're holding?"

"It's called a *Mace*," the man answered.

"Cool," said Thomas, gazing at the sparkling jewels. "What's it for?"

"Well, it's a symbol of the Assembly's authority. They can't actually meet without it."

"Really!"

"Thomas!" Claire called in a loud whisper, motioning for him to come back beside her. He trotted over to Claire. "That must be the Sergeant-at-Arms," she continued. "Miss Phelps said we were the very last."

A man in a three-piece suit came around the corner. He was the Speaker and stood behind the Sergeant-at-

Arms. Then came two ladies in black slacks and jackets. One was carrying a black briefcase and the other a huge leatherbound book. Two young people, about fifteen years old each, followed them wearing the same clothes as Thomas and Claire.

"Now!" commanded Claire. "Behind those Pages."

Thomas followed Claire as she walked over to the other Pages.

"Hi," she said. "I'm Claire and this is my brother Thomas."

"I'm Anna," the Page replied. "This is Sam. Nice to meet you. We haven't worked with you before."

"No," answered Claire, "but we're really looking forward to it."

Thomas opened his mouth to say something when Anna continued. "We're going to be busy tonight. There are only four of us instead of the usual six."

Thomas tugged on his collar. His face was red.

"Get ready, we'll be going into the Chamber right away," explained Anna.

"What chamber?" asked Thomas.

"Not funny," scolded Sam.

The Sergeant-at-Arms spoke in a loud voice. "Order! Order! Mr. Speaker!" He led the way through the door into an immense room. It was full of men and women, each standing quietly behind small wooden desks. There were about fifty people on the Government side of the room and about forty on the Opposition side. Spectators watched from a balcony. The ceiling formed a high arch with ornate woodwork. Dark oak panelling covered the walls and colourful flags hung on long poles along one side.

"Who are all these guys at the desks?" Thomas asked Sam as they walked along the red carpet through the room.

"They're the MLAs," he replied. "Where have you been?"

"What's an MLA?" Thomas whispered.

"Member of the Legislative Assembly." Sam turned slightly as they walked across the Chamber. "Don't you remember your training? You must be new."

"Whatever gave you that idea?" asked Thomas.

"Shhhh!" said Claire.

The Sergeant-at-Arms walked around a table in the middle of the room, placing the Mace on a cushion. He was careful to place it so that the crown on the end faced toward the Government MLAs.

The Sergeant-at-Arms turned and faced an elaborate throne as the Speaker walked over and stood in front of it. The Clerk and the Clerk Assistant stood on either side of the table that held the Mace while Anna and Sam stepped forward to stand by a railing next to the Speaker. Thomas and Claire followed them, but Anna signalled with her eyes for them to stand by the railing on the other side of the Speaker, which they did.

Thomas looked up at the ceiling and the fancy woodwork on the walls. He felt like he was in some kind of palace. The place smelled like furniture polish. Three chandeliers hung from the ceiling. He was in the middle of counting the lights on one of the chandeliers when he heard the Speaker say, "We pray for wisdom and insight as we strive to make this jurisdiction a better place for everyone. Amen."

What was that all about? thought Thomas. Suddenly everyone sat down, except for the Pages.

The Clerk stood up and called out, "Introduction of bills!"

"The Honourable Minister Scott McPhedran from Deep Valley," the Speaker announced, sitting on the throne.

A man with jet black hair stood at his desk on the

right side of the room. "Mr. Speaker," he began in a deep voice, "I want to introduce Bill 512, the Dangerous Driver Taxation Act. The Government believes that this act will help pay for the rising costs associated with people who drive their vehicles dangerously. Over thirteen percent of accidents in the past year were related to drivers who had been previously charged with dangerous driving. It is further known that…"

Just then, Sam walked over to one of the MLAs. The MLA handed him a piece of paper, which Sam took to another MLA sitting at the back of the room. Sam then returned to his place beside the Speaker, but left soon after to deliver a second message.

"Besides this," continued McPhedran, "the medical system will not be subject to the high costs of injuries if the injuries don't happen in the first place. Dangerous drivers will be prevented from driving at all if they are heavily taxed. It is also common knowledge that…"

Thomas couldn't understand what MLA McPhedran was talking about. It reminded him of a law show he'd seen on TV.

Claire suddenly walked over to an MLA holding up a piece of paper. She had observed Sam and figured out what to do. The MLA handed Claire a message with the name "Mary Fitzimmons" written on the folded paper. Claire checked the map Miss Phelps had given her and located Mary Fitzimmons' desk on the other side of the room. Soon after that, Anna picked up a note from an MLA and delivered it. Thomas observed all of this, his head moving back and forth like he was watching a slow tennis game.

This might be fun after all, he thought.

Claire, Anna, and Sam were all gone from their posts, delivering messages to MLAs, when Thomas saw someone hold up a note at the back of the Opposition side of the room. He quickly walked over. A balding man with big bushy eyebrows handed him a message. "Here," he said with a raspy voice. His face looked like he had just eaten a lemon.

Thomas looked at the name on the note and then at his map. The note was for Scott McPhedran, the man who was speaking!

On his way to MLA McPhedran, Thomas accidently dropped the note on the floor. It flipped under an empty desk. He crawled under the desk and, seeing the note was open, read it. It said, in big letters:

SIT   DOWN   MCPHEDRAN

THIS   TAXATION   BILL   IS   STUPID

SO   GO   FLY   A   KITE

JEFF   REIMER

Thomas glanced back at the lemon-faced MLA. *I can't deliver this,* he thought. *This is really rude!* He scratched his head, then his armpit, wondering what to do.

He sat on the floor studying the note. Jeff Reimer wrote in capitals, with odd spaces between the letters.

I know!

Thomas picked up a pencil from the empty desk and crawled back underneath. He erased a couple of letters, added a word, and wrote some letters in spaces. He tried to make his writing look like Reimer's. When he finished, the note read:

WELL DONE McPHEDRAN

THIS TAXATION BILL IS LIKE CUPID

WHO GOES FLY A KITE

JEFF REIMER

Thomas wasn't sure about the last bit about the kite, but thought the message didn't sound quite as bad as it had.

"The Honourable Opposition Member from Pendleton South, Wallace Whitney," the Speaker announced.

A man stood up just a few desks away from Jeff Reimer.

"Mr. Speaker, we oppose this bill," Whitney began, "because dangerous driving is already addressed through the Traffic Act. By adding this additional level of taxation, there could be..."

Thomas delivered his note to McPhedran and when he returned to his place by the railing, he saw the puzzled look on McPhedran's face. McPhedran ran his fingers through his thick black hair, wrote a note, and held it up. Claire walked over and picked it up. Thomas watched her deliver the message to Jeff Reimer, who stared at McPhedran after he read it.

When Claire returned to her place, Thomas whispered, "What did that last note say?"

"How I am supposed to know? I never read it! We're supposed to deliver messages, not read them, Thomas. Look! It's your turn now. Hurry up and get the note Mr. Reimer is holding."

While Thomas walked to Mr. Reimer, the Speaker announced the name of someone on the Government side of the room who began talking. Thomas picked up the note from Jeff Reimer. Once again, it was addressed to Scott McPhedran.

Thomas began his trek across the Chamber. What did the note say? Dare he look at it? Could he take a quick peek without anyone noticing? Suddenly there were a lot of MLAs pounding their hands on their desktops, applauding whoever had spoken. The noise thundered in the cavernous room and was enough of a distraction that Thomas took a quick look at the note in his hands. It read:

LISTEN   Mc PHEDRAN

QUIT   THIS GOOFY TALK

ABOUT   CUPID AND COME TO

YOUR   SENSES. WE'LL BEAT

YOU   ANYWAY.

JEFF REIMER

Thomas bent down to pretend he was doing up his shoelace, which, as it turned out, he actually needed to do. Stealing the pencil off a desk whose MLA had his back turned, Thomas quickly erased and added some letters to the note. It only took a moment. He wished he knew how to spell better. When he finished, the note read:

LISTEN   MC PHEDRAN

QUITE THE   LOFTY TALK

ABOUT CUPID,   COME TO

YOUR   FENSES. WE'LL MEAT

YOU HALFWAY.

JEFF REIMER

Thomas nodded as he read what was now written, got up, and walked across the room to McPhedran. He handed him the note.

When Thomas reached the railing beside the Speaker, he glanced over at McPhedran. The man's mouth was open as he gazed across the Chamber at Reimer. He furiously wrote a note and held it in the air. Sam picked it up and made the delivery.

Thomas and Claire both had to deliver notes right after that, then the Speaker announced, "The Chamber will now adjourn for a fifteen-minute recess."

Immediately the room filled with conversation as the MLAs began milling about. Some MLAs left the room.

"What happens now?" Thomas asked Sam.

"Well, you can go get a drink or use the bathroom. We don't have anything to do for fifteen minutes. Just be back here on time."

Claire took Thomas' arm. "Thomas, I saw you writing on a message. What was that all about?"

Thomas' eyes got wide and he stuck a finger in his collar to see if he could loosen it. "Well, I, uh... nothing really, you know, just, uh... Hey, let's go get a drink! Maybe we can find the Transporter. Don't you think we've, you know, had enough fun already? This has sure been fun, but whatdya say we go?" He walked toward the door they had come through earlier.

Claire put her hands on her hips and frowned, then followed Thomas out of the Chamber. When they reached the hallway, they were greeted by Miss Phelps.

"So, how has it been going? Everything ticketyboo?"

Thomas looked at Claire for a translation, but Claire simply said, "Yes, everything is fine."

"I hear there are some real challenges with the proposed legislation," continued Miss Phelps. "Remember to keep focused and don't let anything distract you from delivering the messages. The notes you deliver convey critical information which is why *you* are instrumental in helping to ensure that good decisions come out of these sessions."

"Right you are!" Thomas agreed, shifting his weight from one foot to the other.

Miss Phelps looked at him for a moment. "Just think, one day you'll be able to tell your children how you played a small but very important part in the democratic process!" She had a big smile on her face.

Thomas smiled weakly and asked where the bathroom was. "I'll be back in a minute."

"Don't be tardy," said Miss Phelps. "The session begins again in twelve minutes."

Thomas was surprised at the high ceiling in the bathroom. The floor and counters were made of marble and the doorknobs were brass. He went into a cubicle so he could blow his nose. Just then, two men came into the bathroom, talking fast and loud.

"Listen, McPhedran, why ever do we need to talk in here?" asked a man with a raspy voice. "What in the world do you have to say to me that can't be said out in the hallway?"

"Because you're writing such cryptic messages," said a deep voice. "Jeff, just tell me outright. Are you serious about meeting us halfway on this bill?"

"That depends if you continue confusing politics with cupid," answered the raspy voice.

"Me! You're the one who brought up the cupid thing in the first place!"

The two men stood in silence for a moment, staring at each other. Thomas opened the cubicle door a crack and saw Scott McPhedran run his fingers through his thick black hair. "Listen, Reimer," he said, "this bill will only pass—"

"If you get the Opposition on side with you," interrupted Reimer. "And you will, if you recognize that most aspects of it are already covered by the Traffic Act. By simply proposing changes to the Traffic Act to cover your new requirements, you'll get what you want, and so will we." Reimer's bushy eyebrows went up and down a few times.

McPhedran rubbed his chin. "I think I see what you mean. Okay. So this is what you meant by coming to the fence and meeting us halfway."

Reimer was about to say something when a voice from a speaker in the ceiling announced, "Ladies and gentlemen, the session will resume in eight minutes."

Reimer blinked a few times. "If you can go with amending the Traffic Act, as opposed to creating new legislation, we'll be on side with you."

McPhedran nodded.

"It'll work," Reimer continued, patting McPhedran on the back. "I'm sure this will be easily accepted by my colleagues. Now, come on, let's go!"

"Well, what if they don't accept it? And what if *my* colleagues won't agree to such a radical proposal?"

"I'm sure your explanation of the benefits to all parties will win them over."

McPhedran and Reimer shook hands as they left the bathroom. They had only walked a few steps before Reimer said, "Let's call for an extension to the recess. How about fifteen more minutes?"

"Good idea."

Thomas waited, then followed a safe distance behind the two MLAs. When he got close to the Chamber, he was surprised to see everyone filing out into the hallway. He moved to one side with his back against the wall and saw Sam on the other side.

"What's happening?" called Thomas.

"There's been a request to extend the recess another fifteen minutes! If this keeps up, we'll be here all night!" he joked.

I certainly hope not! thought Thomas.

He noticed the Government MLAs filing into a room down the hall while the Opposition MLAs headed in the other direction. Loud voices echoed off the high ceiling of the arched hallway. Some Members waved their arms as they spoke.

When the hallway cleared, Claire came out of the Chamber and saw Thomas. She quickly walked over to him. "Thomas, I've been looking for the Transporter. Have you seen it anywhere?"

"No, but I wouldn't mind finding it sooner than later! How about a phone? Have you seen a phone anywhere?"

Claire studied him. "Thomas, stop fidgeting. Is there something you should be telling me?"

"Yes! No! Uh, Claire? Could you go to that room down the hall on the left and just kinda listen to what's going on?"

"You mean eavesdrop? Thomas! You know I wouldn't do that."

"No, no, of course not. I was just kidding. Uh... how

about just standing outside the door in case someone has a message for you to deliver, and while you're at it... just listen to anything that, you know, might be said. I'll meet you back here in a few minutes."

Thomas turned and paced down the hall until he found the room occupied by the Government MLAs. His shoes made no noise on the polished granite floor. He crept up to the dark oak door and put his ear against it.

"That's preposterous!" shouted someone in the room. "We can't possibly allow such a manoeuvre by the Opposition. It's unheard of!"

"It may be a first, but why not consider the potential outcome? It could benefit everyone!" called out another.

"Ah, but that's the issue!" responded someone else. "When has the Opposition ever done anything that has benefited both us and them? I say they're being devious. They must have a hidden agenda!"

"But what? Whatever could it be? This proposal to meet halfway and... Scott, what did the note say?"

"I have it right here in my pocket," said a deep voice. "Here, take a look yourself."

There was the sound of unfolding paper, then someone read:

Listen McPhedran.
Quite the lofty talk about cupid. Come to your fenses.
We'll meat you halfway.
Jeff Reimer

There was a pause, then, "McPhedran, what's this stuff about cupid mean? And surely Reimer knows how to spell—he spelt *fences* and *meet* incorrectly!"

There were some chuckles. Thomas' face flushed. Tingles of sweat on his back made it itchy.

"I don't know what the reference to cupid means," puzzled McPhedran. "His first note, which I don't have with me, said something about cupid flying a kite. Very cryptic. Very strange. Reimer has always been difficult to understand and unwilling to talk things over. Now he seems quite conciliatory. Wanting to work with us. I responded to his first note by asking what cupid had to do with the Traffic Act. I responded to his second note where he asked us to meet them halfway by saying I wanted to know more about what he was thinking. We discussed the matter during the break. He seems quite intent on supporting a revision to the Traffic Act without initiating any new legislation."

There was silence for a moment, then McPhedran continued. "This is the first time in a very long time that anything from Jeff Reimer has made any political sense, notwithstanding his reference to cupid. Very strange. Very strange, indeed."

There were some chuckles, then someone blurted, "Or maybe cupid has shot his arrow into Jeff Reimer, making him fall in love with the political process!"

There was loud laughter. Someone added, "Or maybe he's fallen in love with us, the Government!"

Uproarious laughter followed, the kind where, even if you don't know what's funny, you start to laugh along. Thomas laughed a little, then cleared his throat and thought it might be a good time to find Claire. He met her in the hallway.

"Did you hear anything, Claire?" he asked.

"Well, sort of. There was a lot of talk about cupid and revising the Traffic Act or something. I could only hear bits and pieces. There was a lot of laughing. Sometimes they seemed to laugh for ages. Thomas, what has cupid got to do with the Traffic Act?"

"Well now, that's a very good question," replied

Thomas, brushing some lint off his jacket. "It's one of those things about politics that, you know, is, uh, rather unusual. Rather unconventional." Thomas scrunched his shoulders and rubbed his back against the wall. "Claire, let's look for the Transporter, shall we?"

"Oh, there you are!" came a voice from behind them. It was Miss Phelps. "I've been looking all over for you. The session will resume shortly. Do you need permission from your parents to stay later? We'll arrange for transportation home afterward."

"No. Thank you, Miss Phelps. We'll be fine," answered Claire.

"There is one thing," added Thomas.

Miss Phelps peered over her glasses. "Yes, and what may that be?"

He forced a smile. "I've lost something and I'm wondering if there is a 'Lost and Found' somewhere?"

"Well, there is, but perhaps you would be so kind as to tell me what you have misplaced?"

"Sure. It's a Transporter that—"

"That looks like a block of wood with two eggbeaters sticking out of it," interrupted Claire.

"I see," said Miss Phelps, frowning. "And what would you be doing with such a thing in the Legislature?"

"Well, that's a little more difficult to explain," said Thomas. "But have you seen it?"

"As a matter of fact, yes. The janitorial staff just emptied the garbage cans in the Chamber and an object, similar to the one you described, was in one."

"Where? Where is it now?" asked Thomas earnestly.

"My guess is that it's in the dumpster outside," she explained, pointing down the hallway. As Thomas and Claire started to run, Miss Phelps called after them, "The session will begin shortly, so don't be late. It could prove to be very interesting."

"I'm sure it will," called Thomas over his shoulder.

Thomas and Claire ran down the hall until they saw a grey-haired janitor pushing a broom.

"Can you tell us where the dumpster is?" asked Claire.

The janitor pointed to a stairwell. "Down those stairs and to your right."

They ran down three flights of stairs, burst through a door leading outside, and saw a blue dumpster full of green trash bags. A garbage truck approached with big forks in front ready to lift it.

"Claire, stop the driver while I dig around inside," yelled Thomas.

"How am I supposed to do that?" asked Claire frantically.

"I don't know." Thomas' eyes narrowed. "Pretend the Transporter is that music box you got from Auntie Brenda last Christmas."

Claire's eyes grew large. She ran down the steps by the loading dock, hurtled over a garbage can lying on its side, then jumped over a mud puddle before stopping in front of the truck.

The truck driver rolled down his window when he saw Claire's Olympic effort. "Hey, where's the fire?" he asked.

"Could I ask you to wait just a minute? My brother lost something and thinks it might be in the dumpster."

"Well, tell him to make it fast, sweetie. I'm on a schedule, you know."

Thomas felt the outside of two or three garbage bags. "This is going to be hopeless," he said to himself as he tore open a bag. Then, to his surprise, he saw two eggbeaters poking through the side of another bag. He wrenched the Transporter free, jumped clear of the dumpster, and waved to the truck driver.

Claire carefully walked around the mud puddle and garbage can, then up the steps by the loading dock. She put her hand on Thomas' shoulder.

Just before he pushed the Activator, they heard a loud noise from an open window above them. It sounded like the MLAs thumping their hands on their desks, mixed with loud laughter. Thomas turned to Claire with a half-smile and pushed the Activator.

The air started to rush past them as they somersaulted in slow motion. The rumble of the truck engine faded, as did the laughter from the window above. For a while it was quiet, except for the sound of a high-pitched siren.

Then came an explosion. Another explosion was louder and closer. Thomas landed hard on broken concrete, as did Claire. A third, even larger explosion nearby blew rocks and dust into the air. Thomas and Claire covered their heads with their hands. Their ears rang as rocks and dirt rained down.

Discussion Questions

Describe how Thomas and Claire each felt about being in the Legislature.

Thomas and Claire had completely different responses to the same situation. Is either response right or wrong? How should you treat other people who react or respond to situations differently from you?

What ideas do you have for coping when you find yourself in an uncomfortable situation? For example, suddenly being asked to play the piano at a family reunion, needing to apologize to a neighbour for accidently breaking their window with your baseball, or being asked to dance with your cousin at a relative's wedding (and you don't know how to dance...)?

Although Thomas had good intentions, do you think he should have changed the notes from MLA Jeff Reimer?

At the end of the chapter, Thomas and Claire were transported to a new location. Where do you think they are now?

Thomas

Claire

chapter 6

When Claire opened her eyes, the air was thick with dust. She coughed several times. She could hear the *rat-a-tat-tat* of a machine gun somewhere. She had landed awkwardly on some rubble and badly sprained her ankle. She sat up as pain seared through her leg. She took a deep breath, dragged herself to a broken concrete wall nearby and put her back against it. That's when she saw Thomas. He was sitting on the ground near a burned-out car. His eyes were squeezed shut.

"Thomas, are you alright?"

"Yeah," he answered slowly, sitting up and rubbing his right knee. "Just landed a bit hard. I'll… I'll be okay."

A whistling sound above them grew progressively louder, ending with a massive explosion about three hundred meters away. Thomas and Claire put their heads down and squeezed their hands against their ears. After a few moments, a hailstorm of rocks and dirt pummelled the ground. As quickly as he could, Thomas shuffled over to Claire and they grabbed hold of each other. The wall they leaned against had part of a cracked roof over it, the remains of a small building. It provided some protection.

"Where are we, Thomas?" asked Claire frantically, scanning the remains of what had been a small town.

"I don't know! But we've got to get out of here fast!"

They heard another whistling sound, this time further away. The resulting blast still shook the ground under them. Claire snuggled closer to Thomas and noticed his rapid breathing.

Then came the sporadic popping sound of gunfire. Thomas' pulse throbbed in his neck. Claire trembled. Every so often, a bullet whizzed through the air over their heads. A building burned about a kilometer away. Thick black smoke billowed into the air.

"Do you think Mom and Dad are worried about us?" asked Claire quietly.

"We don't even know if they've noticed we're missing."

"We've been gone long enough," Claire moaned, taking quick, shallow breaths. "Surely they miss us."

Thomas didn't know what to say. He rubbed his sore knee. "I'm sure they do."

Claire nodded, then out of the corner of her eye saw the Transporter. It was almost a football field away in an open area to their right, atop the remains of a wall. If it had been night, she wouldn't have seen it; even in daylight, it was hard to see, surrounded as it was by pieces of wood and blocks of odd-shaped rocks and other debris.

Thomas got up to get it, but Claire held him back. "Thomas, it's not safe. You could get shot by someone."

"What makes this spot any safer? We gotta go. It's the only way," persisted Thomas. He limped for about five meters, then hit the ground as a fast whistling sound sliced the air, followed by an explosion that hurt their ears. They both lay on the ground shaking, hands over their heads. Bits of rock fell all around them, some bouncing off nearby walls. The air smelled like burning matches.

When the dust cleared a little, Thomas turned around. "Are you okay, Claire?"

"Yes. I guess so," she sobbed, squeezing as tight as possible to the wall. Tears ran down her cheeks. "Thomas, if we got killed or something, what would actually happen to us? I mean, would we end up at home right away, or—"

"I don't know." Thomas took a deep breath. He felt blood trickle down his face. "Claire! I'm bleeding!"

"How bad?"

He sat up, his back to Claire, and using his sleeve to wipe the blood determined it wasn't a bad cut. His gaze settled on the building across the street. "Look, Claire! There's something on that wall!"

"Where?"

"See that ledge partway up?"

"Yes! What is it?"

"Some kind of box. It has a red cross on it. It might be useful. Should I get it?"

"How bad are you bleeding?"

"I could use a bandage. I'm gonna go get it." He got to his feet and, keeping low, hobbled through an obstacle course of bricks and fragments of wood.

He rested when he got to the wall. It was riddled with bullet holes. On a ledge high off the ground were two metal boxes, each larger than a shoebox. He couldn't reach them. He looked for something to stand on, but there were only big slabs of broken concrete.

"Claire, come and help me," he called.

Using a stick she'd found as a crutch, Claire staggered across the street to Thomas. She lifted the boxes down and handed them to Thomas one at a time.

They sat down when they finally got back to their shelter and pried the lids off. Each box had a blanket and a bottle of water. Claire's also had a first aid kit. She took out a bandage and placed it over the cut on Thomas' cheek.

Thomas took the water bottle out of his box.

Claire suddenly looked to her left, then her right. "Did you hear that?" she asked quickly.

"What?"

"That. There it is again!"

"What? All I hear is ringing."

"Listen! Carefully!"

They sat in silence for a few moments, then Claire stood painfully to her feet.

"There!" She raised her arm and pointed across the street, past where they had found the survival kits. "Over there, Thomas! By that broken tree! There's a little boy coming this way!"

Thomas looked where Claire pointed and saw the boy, about six years old, stumbling toward them. He was about twenty meters away when Thomas heard what he couldn't before. The boy was whimpering.

"Hey! Come over here!" Thomas called.

The boy stopped and stared for a moment. He shivered, then stumbled toward them.

When he reached them, Thomas and Claire saw that he was filthy. Tears streaked his dirty cheeks. One leg of his pants had been burned, but Claire could see that his skin had been spared.

He collapsed on the ground in front of them.

Without hesitation, Claire took her blanket and laid it out beside the boy, then helped him move onto one half of it. "Thomas," she said, "give him a drink from your water bottle."

Thomas hesitated. "What if... what if I might need it?"

"Then you can have mine."

Thomas looked at Claire thoughtfully, then opened

the lid. He gently lifted the boy's head and put the bottle near his mouth. The boy drank slowly at first. Little sips. Then he sat up a little and drank and drank and drank. The bottle was half empty when he lay down again. Claire tenderly covered him with the rest of the blanket and he fell asleep. Thomas put the cap on the bottle and placed it by the boy's head.

It was getting dark and Thomas realized there hadn't been any gunshots or bomb blasts for a while. There was a strange quiet. The air was turning cool.

"Claire, I'm gonna get the Transporter. Do you think it's dark enough to be safe? But if it gets any darker, I won't be able to see it."

"I think you should go when it's a little darker. Even if it's hard to find, you won't be so obvious a target. Wait a few more minutes. Let's just rest for now."

Thomas nodded and got out his blanket. He spread it on the ground near the wall and said, "Sit next to me. We'll wrap this thing around us."

Claire crept over to the soundly sleeping boy, gently stroked his hair, and tucked the blanket around his body.

She handed him her water bottle. "Here, have a drink."

Thomas held the bottle for a moment, then handed it back. "You first."

Claire took a long drink, then passed the bottle to Thomas who normally would have made a big deal of wiping the mouth of the bottle on his sleeve. This time, he just took a drink. A very grateful drink.

They sat together under the blanket, their backs against the wall. Claire snuggled over and they soon fell fast asleep.

The sound of an earth-shattering bomb blast shocked Thomas and Claire out of their troubled dreams. It was louder than any thunderclap they had ever heard. The earth shook so hard that part of the building across the street crumbled from the vibrations.

Claire hugged Thomas tightly. "Let's get out of here before we get hurt!"

They noticed the little boy was no longer there.

"He's taken the blanket!" exclaimed Thomas. "And the water!"

"I'm sure he needed them more than we did," said Claire thoughtfully, still clinging to Thomas.

The sun was already high in the sky. Instead of a little rest and a twilight trek to the Transporter, they had slept for hours—and now it was daytime again. Thomas felt frantic, like he did on those days when he overslept his alarm and missed the school bus.

A low whistling sound knifed the air. There was quiet, then a vibrating explosion about a kilometer away. More gunfire and then six bomb blasts in a row. Each one seemed closer than the last.

Claire shivered.

"It's now or never!" yelled Thomas as he leaped to his feet. His knee hurt, so he ran slowly. He crossed the street and turned toward the field.

He hadn't gone fifty meters when he nearly collided with a woman coming around the corner of a building. She was shorter than Thomas and her stringy hair was tied back in a red scarf. Her clothes were ragged and she had a walking stick.

They both yelped in shock at seeing each other, then a bomb flew so close overhead that Thomas thought it would hit the building beside them. It sped past and exploded on the other side as he and the woman both fell to the ground and covered their heads. Big chunks of rock landed all around them. A small piece hit the back of Thomas' right leg. Some larger ones hit the woman.

Thomas' tongue stuck to the roof of his mouth. After a minute, waiting to see if more chunks would fall, he lifted himself to his knees. Breathing rapidly, he rubbed his aching leg where it had been hit. The woman lay still, then struggled to get up, blood streaming down her face. Thomas had seen blood before, but not this much. He helped her to her feet and saw that her left arm was twisted awkwardly.

"Come with me," he said as she leaned on him.

They carefully made their way over to Claire.

"*Herarechi,*" the woman uttered in a low breathless voice when they reached Claire. "*Herarechi.*"

"I don't understand," Claire said softly. She sat the lady down, opened the first aid kit, then wiped blood from her head. Claire remembered the time her cousin Luke had run into the corner of her Aunty Cathy's china cabinet and got a gash on his forehead. Although it bled all over his face, the actual cut was small. Claire hoped that was the case with this woman, and was relieved when she found the cut on the front edge of the woman's scalp. It was deep but not very large. Claire found a piece of gauze and placed it over the cut.

"Thomas. Hold this piece of gauze here," she ordered.

Thomas pressed gently on the gauze. "Something's wrong with her left arm," he observed.

The woman winced as she held her arm against her stomach.

"It might be broken," Claire said, "but whether it's broken or not, at least I can splint it and put it in a sling. I know that much from the first aid class I took last spring. Thomas, do you see anything that might work as a splint?"

Thomas looked around, still holding the gauze in place. "No, I don't... Hey! Yes! Over here by this wall."

With his free hand, he gestured toward a piece of wood about as long as a ruler. It was smooth on one side.

"That'll do," she said with a nod, picking it up and rubbing off the dirt. She positioned the splint on the woman's arm and used adhesive tape to hold it in place.

Next, she got a large cloth out of the first aid kit and folded it to make a triangle. She suspended her own arm in the cloth and held the corners near her neck to show the woman. Then she gently placed the cloth under the woman's left arm. Claire watched the woman's face carefully as she lifted both ends of the cloth around the woman's neck.

"There's not enough to tie these ends together," Claire said. She thought for a moment. "Maybe there's a pin in the first aid kit." She rummaged around in the kit. "Hey, here's one! And a chocolate bar!"

"Bonus!" cheered Thomas, his eyes widening.

"First things first," said Claire, pinning the sling with the safety pin. She removed the blood-soaked gauze Thomas held and examined the cut. The bleeding had stopped. "Good. Thomas, break that chocolate bar into three pieces while I put a bandage on this cut."

"Ten-four," said Thomas enthusiastically.

Claire put some antibiotic ointment on the cut and a butterfly bandage. "There, that's got it," she said confidently once she had finished. The woman smiled slightly.

Thomas tried to break the chocolate bar into three equal pieces, but one piece ended up being larger than the other two. He eyed the pieces thoughtfully and presented them to the woman to choose.

She looked at the chocolate, at Thomas and Claire, whispered "*Herarechi*," and took a piece.

"That must mean 'thank you' in whatever language she speaks," suggested Thomas. He examined the two pieces that remained, one of them being the large one. He offered them to Claire, hoping she too would take a smaller piece. She did. Thomas' shoulders relaxed as he stuffed the last piece in his mouth.

"*Herarechi*," said the woman again, nodding to Thomas and Claire. She got up slowly and began to walk away, carefully choosing her path amongst the rocks and debris.

"Should we follow her?" asked Claire. "Maybe she knows where it's safe."

"No, we need to get the Transporter and get out of here. First I want to check my box. Maybe there's a chocolate bar in there I didn't notice earlier." He dug around for a moment. "Hey, I got one too!" But he frowned as he pulled out what was inside. It was a small pair of binoculars. He sighed, turning them around in his hands. "Well, they're nice, but definitely not edible."

Thomas stood and held the binoculars to his eyes. The Transporter still sat on the broken wall in the open field to their right. He scanned the terrain to select the route he would take and had just decided which way to go when a low-pitched whistling sound far to their left shattered the air.

Thomas and Claire ducked behind some broken slabs of concrete. The shell exploded against a windowless three-story building and blew it to pieces. Only one wall remained standing in the billowing dust.

Thomas, crouching, looked at the wall through the binoculars. As the air cleared, his eyes froze on something.

"Hey! There's someone over there! At the bottom of that wall! They're... they're covered in rubble!"

"Let me see," demanded Claire, grabbing the binoculars. It took her a while to locate the person. "It's not one person. There's a man and a child. Thomas, go help them!"

Before he could answer, gunfire splintered their thoughts. Bullets ricocheted off the building across the street. Thomas and Claire fell to the ground and covered their heads with their hands. More bullets zipped by, then stopped.

Thomas shuddered. "Why me? Why should I go? I'm not going way over there!"

"I would if I could walk better. You at least can limp. Maybe you can help them!"

"Are you kidding? They must be two hundred meters away!"

"What's that got to do with anything?"

"Well, they're too far away to help. We already helped that boy and that lady. That's enough! They were close by. I'm not going to risk my life to help someone that far away." He pointed to the man and child. "Besides, it's open between here and there. I might get shot. Then what?"

"Thomas!" Claire responded sternly. "Those people are no further away than the Transporter, and the way to the Transporter is as much in the open as it is to those people."

"What are you saying?"

"I'm saying that the likelihood of getting shot is probably the same either way."

"That's a pleasant thought!"

"Well, what would you prefer to be known for? That you died trying to save somebody else or you died trying to save yourself?"

"Neither, actually."

A barrage of bullets whizzed by, pockmarking the nearby buildings.

Thomas and Claire lay on the ground, silent, as tears ran down their cheeks.

Two simultaneous bomb blasts, perhaps a kilometer

away, vibrated the air. Then two more, a little further still. Then it was quiet.

Thomas wiped his face with his sleeve and sat up. "Okay. I'll go. The bombs seem a little further away right now." He took a deep breath, then licked his dry lips. "What should my plan be?"

"Tie your shoelaces first."

"Right." Thomas tied them as tight as he could.

"Here," directed Claire. "Take the blanket, first aid kit, and leftover water."

"Won't we need any of that stuff?"

"No," said Claire firmly. She watched as he gathered the supplies in his arms, as well as the binoculars. "Be careful!"

Thomas gave her a half-smile. He limped away, carefully choosing his path, keeping low, and looking around for any movement. A shell landed in the distance and he saw another building slowly collapse. A light breeze blew thick smoke toward him. He heard the faint popping of gunfire somewhere.

After what seemed like forever, Thomas reached the man and child, a little girl about two years old. Staccato sobs mingled with her hoarse cries. Thomas was relieved to see no blood.

"Hi," he said, crouching down. "What's your name?"

The girl sobbed with big gasps, tears streaming down her cheeks. Her dirty dress was torn. She seemed unhurt but frightened.

Thomas turned his attention to the man. He was conscious, but his face writhed in pain. He looked like he was yelling, but no sound came out of his mouth. His legs were buried in broken concrete. Thomas was afraid of what he might see, but carefully lifted the chunks of rock away. He couldn't budge one heavy piece.

He found a timber about two meters long and used it

to pry the slab of concrete off the man's legs. As Thomas lifted it up, the man slid out from underneath, pushing with all his might.

Breathing rapidly, he whispered, "*Herarechi.*"

"You're welcome."

Gunfire suddenly peppered the wall behind them and a shell exploded less than a hundred meters away. Thomas fell to the ground, the pressure from the blast hurting his ears so badly that he felt nauseous. The little girl shrieked uncontrollably.

Thomas bit his bottom lip and got to his feet. While the air was thick with dust, he put his shoulder under the man's left arm, helping him to stand. He picked up the little girl with his other arm and trudged to a small building about twenty meters away. It was no bigger than a garden shed, with a partial roof and no door. They had just gotten inside when a bomb blasted the wall where they had just been. Chunks of concrete flew through the air, some falling through the roof and onto the floor below, narrowly missing the little girl. The man tried in vain to calm her.

Another blast some distance away shook the ground like an earthquake.

That one sounded like it might have hit the Transporter, Thomas thought. He squinted and turned his head. *Maybe even landed... near Claire!*

Thomas took his blanket and wrapped it around the man and the girl. He detected some scrapes and cuts on the man's legs where his pants had been ripped, but they didn't appear to be broken—at least as far as Thomas could tell.

He searched through the first aid kit and found a bottle of pain killers. He read the label, then took out two tablets and handed them to the man along with the water bottle. The man understood, swallowed the pills, and took a drink, then helped the girl have a drink.

"*Herarechi,*" the man whispered. The little girl cuddled against the man's chest. She no longer cried but occasionally took a quick sobbing breath.

Thomas took the binoculars and threw the strap around his neck. He dropped the first aid kit on the ground beside the man and took a deep breath.

"Goodbye."

He disappeared out the door.

It took a long time to get back to Claire as there were more chunks of concrete and rubble strewn over the ground. Thomas was so relieved to see Claire that he gave her a bear hug and didn't let go for a long time. He then pulled out his binoculars to search for the Transporter. It was gone! It was no longer on the broken wall. In fact, the wall was no longer there. A gaping hole was left in its place.

"Claire!" he shouted. "The Transporter is—"

"Is right here," she finished, holding it up for him to see.

Thomas blew the air out of his lungs with a huge sigh. "How did you...?"

"I found a torn shirt by the wall and used it to wrap my ankle. I hobbled over and got the Transporter while you were helping those people." She traced her route with a shaking finger. "I just got back when a bomb blew the wall it was sitting on to smithereens. My ears are still ringing."

Thomas raised his eyebrows. "That's scary!" He stared at her for a moment, then smiled. "You're awesome!"

A bomb landed a kilometer away.

"Let's get out of here, now!" cried Thomas. "Put your hand on my shoulder!"

Claire did and Thomas pushed the Activator. Nothing happened. He pushed it again. Still nothing.

"Why does it do this?" asked Claire, a worried look on her face. A faint whistling sound came toward them.

"Quick!" she yelled. "Hurry! Hurry!"

Thomas hit the Transporter with his fist and pushed the Activator a third time. The whistling sound shrieked closer and closer. He pushed the Activator again and again.

A moment later, they found themselves slowly somersaulting through the air. The whistling sound became louder, then softer and softer. There was a faint explosion somewhere far away. The air became cooler.

After some time had passed, they began to hear cheering. The cheering grew louder and louder until it was almost deafening.

Suddenly, Thomas landed on a bench. Something covered his eyes.

Claire landed on a seat somewhere else, beside a lady in a fur coat. Surprised, the lady dropped her cup of coffee on Claire's shoes.

"Oh, I'm so sorry," she exclaimed. "Wherever did you come from?"

Discussion Questions

What is life like for people caught in a war?

Describe the people Thomas and Claire helped, and how they helped them.

Whether people are far away or close by, we can't help everyone who needs it, so how do you decide who to help?

At the end of the chapter, Thomas and Claire were transported to a new location. Where do you think they are now?

chapter 7

Thomas tried to remove whatever was covering his eyes, but a strap under his chin held it in place. Then he realized it was a helmet of some sort and he couldn't move it because he was wearing huge gloves. He took off one glove and pushed the helmet up so he could see: he was seated on one end of a bench in an ice arena with seven other boys. They all wore white hockey jerseys with "Cougars" written across the front in big red letters.

The crowd stopped cheering and began chanting, "Moo-vers, Moo-vers, Moo-vers" when the scoreboard changed. It read "Home 2, Visitors 0."

Thomas decided he was on the visiting team, based on the dejected looks of the other Cougars. He tried moving his sore leg, discovering in the process that it no longer hurt. Then he realized he didn't know where Claire was. He felt strange sitting on the bench in a hockey arena, considering where he had just come from.

A huge crowd filled the bleachers. Thomas couldn't see Claire anywhere. He wondered what he should do when the boy on his left said, "Thomas, pass the water."

Surprised the boy knew his name, Thomas turned and stared. The boy had freckles all over his face and tufts of red hair poked out of the ventilation holes in his helmet. Thomas saw a water bottle on the ledge in front of him and passed it to the boy.

"Kevin?" asked the boy on Thomas' right. "Why are you drinking water? You shouldn't be thirsty! We haven't played at all this whole period or the last one. And with the score two to nothing, we're not gonna be playing the rest of the game." He was skinny with black-rimmed glasses. His helmet was too big and he had a large pimple on the end of his nose. Thomas saw the number 11 on his sleeve.

"Dennis, why is it we aren't playing?" Kevin sounded sarcastic.

"Because you never pass the puck."

"No," disagreed Kevin. "Because you're useless."

Thomas was about to say something when the Cougars' coach, a bald man with a full moustache and a tight leather jacket, called out, "Line Three, you're on."

Thomas didn't move.

"Come on! Let's get out there!" Kevin yelled, jumping over the boards. Dennis opened the gate and skated onto the ice.

Thomas followed him. He knew how to play hockey but, distracted by the crowd, he didn't know where to go or what to do.

Why should it matter that all these people are watching? he asked himself.

He saw Kevin head to center ice for the faceoff. Dennis skated awkwardly to right wing, so Thomas proceeded to left wing. The scoreboard showed two minutes left in the second period. The right winger facing Thomas had a blue jersey with "Movers" written in italicized orange letters. Thomas didn't like the sneer on the boy's face.

The referee dropped the puck and Kevin passed it to Thomas. Thomas skated toward the Mover goalie but lost control of the puck. A Mover player quickly shot it back down the ice toward the Cougars' end. Thomas chased the play around for a while, then realized he was skating in circles, watching what was going on. He was also out of position.

What am I doing on right wing?

Suddenly, the puck slid along the boards toward him. He turned and saw a Mover defenseman between him and the Mover goalie. Thomas banked the puck off the boards, skated the other way around the defenseman, then stickhandled the puck and headed for the net. Another Mover player skated toward him from the corner. Thomas faked a shot, took two more strides, then lifted the puck high into the net above the goalies' glove hand. The referee blew his whistle.

Thomas had scored! Two to one! Surprised, the crowd began to cheer as they realized the Cougars had actually scored.

Back on the bench, Thomas breathed fast.

"Nice shot!" encouraged Kevin.

"Thanks." Thomas took a few more breaths and had a drink of water. He turned toward Dennis. "Hey Dennis, I have an idea."

"What?"

"The next time I get the puck, skate for the net as fast as you can."

Dennis stared at Thomas. "Yeah right!"

"No, I'm serious. Then I'll take a shot and you get the rebound. Or if I don't have a clear shot, I'll pass to you and you can score."

"Yeah right," Dennis repeated. "I doubt we'll play again this period." He looked up at the clock, which showed fifty-nine seconds left. "And if we do, I probably won't even get near the puck."

"Well, if you won't try, you're right," said Thomas.

He gave Dennis a gentle punch on the shoulder as the coach called, "Okay Line Three, let's do it again."

Kevin, Dennis, and Thomas all jumped over the boards. The faceoff was just outside the Mover's blue line. As Thomas skated past Dennis, he said, "Remember, head for the net."

At the faceoff, Kevin slapped the puck to the right defenseman, who passed it to the left defenseman and over to Thomas. Thomas raced down the left side and crossed the blue line. He deked around the Mover's defenseman and saw, out of the corner of his eye, Dennis skating toward the net. He made a perfect pass across the goal crease right to Dennis' stick. Dennis took a slap shot on the open net, missed the puck, tripped, fell, and slid into the boards. A Mover defenseman picked up the puck and made a breakaway pass to his forward, who skated over the Cougar blue line, took a wrist shot, and scored a goal.

The referee blew his whistle as the crowd cheered and jumped to their feet. The score was three to one. The Cougar coach changed up the lines.

On the bench, Thomas panted for breath. "Good try, Dennis."

"But next time keep your stick on the ice," suggested Kevin, shaking his head.

The buzzer sounded to end the second period and the players filed to the dressing room.

Just as Thomas stood to leave, a man in the stands at the end of the bench called, "Hey kid." He waved for Thomas to come and speak to him.

Thomas walked over. The man had long sideburns and wore tiny dark glasses. His voice was gruff as he spoke to Thomas from the other side of the glass.

"Listen, kid. Don't pass to Number Eleven again, got it?"

"Why... why not?" asked Thomas, searching the man's face to see if he was kidding.

"Don't be stupid. That kid couldn't score a goal if his life depended on it. You could have scored another goal if you hadn't passed to him. Don't make that mistake again."

The man scowled, turned, and walked away.

In the dressing room, the coach unzipped his jacket and tucked in his shirt around his generous stomach. He paced back and forth, zipping his jacket up and down several times. "Good job, boys! We got a chance at this one. We got a chance, for sure. We can shake these guys. Remember, these Movers are not shakers!"

No one laughed at this last comment. The prospect of the Cougars getting three more goals against the best team in the league was as unlikely as Wayne Gretzky suddenly coming into the dressing room and putting on a Cougars jersey. And everyone knew it.

Thomas tightened his skates. He suddenly remembered he still hadn't seen Claire anywhere and wondered if he should be concerned.

Nah, he said to himself. *She'll be okay.*

The ten-minute break went by quickly. As the time came to return to the ice, the coach said, "One other thing. That was nice passing out there. Keep it up! That's what I want to see." He rubbed his hands together. "Now, go out there and let's get three unanswered goals!"

Several boys rolled their eyes.

The coach clapped his hands, walked over to the dressing room door, and held it open with his foot. "Remember: good passing means good goals. Good goals mean good games. Let's go out there and have a good game!"

No one moved or said anything. The coach pulled his jacket together so he could zip it up. A couple of boys stood and walked to the door. One by one, the rest of the team followed.

Line One got a goal in the first five minutes of the third period when the puck deflected off a Mover skate and slid past the goalie into the net. Three to two.

About midway through the period, Line Three was back on the ice and Thomas got a breakaway. He used a trick his dad had once taught him. Just before he got to the net, he faked to the left, looked left, then pulled the puck to the right. The goalie went down, his pads sprawling across the goal crease. Just as Thomas began to lift the puck over the goalie's pads, he tripped, slid along the ice, and crashed into the net. It came off its moorings and the referee blew his whistle. Thomas slowly got up and straightened his helmet as Line One came on the ice.

That should've worked, he said to himself.

There were several scoring chances for both teams during the next few minutes. Then, with only three minutes left in the game, the Cougar coach called a timeout.

"Excellent work, boys. Now whatdya think about changing up the lines a little to give us a surprise edge? Whatdya say?"

No one spoke.

Thomas cleared his throat. "Coach, that's a good idea, but… can we keep things as they are? Maybe we could pull our goalie to get the extra skater if we haven't tied the game in the next…" He glanced up at the scoreboard. "…two minutes."

"Good plan," agreed the coach, zipping and unzipping his jacket several times. "Now, keep up that good passing, guys."

The Movers almost scored on the next shift. Then the coach sent Kevin, Dennis, and Thomas deep in their own zone. Kevin took the faceoff and passed to Thomas, who skated up the left side and passed back to Kevin. Back and forth they passed until finally they had a two-on-one. Kevin took a slapshot. The puck bounced off the goalie's pads and onto Thomas' stick. He passed the puck back over to Kevin, who shot again and scored.

Three all! The score was tied! The crowd was on their feet. The Mover fans hadn't expected this. Neither had the Cougar fans, who cheered wildly. The game would now go into overtime, unless someone scored in the remaining twenty seconds.

Thomas skated to the bench, but the coach signalled Line Three to stay on the ice.

The Movers won the faceoff and moved the puck down the ice. A Mover forward stickhandled the puck around Dennis, but at the last moment Dennis poked the puck away and passed it to Kevin. Kevin passed it to Thomas. Thomas had two defensemen rushing toward him, so he sent the puck to Dennis, who was open on right wing. He had a clear shot to the net and took a wild, swinging slapshot. The buzzer sounded to end the third period as the puck feebly hit the boards to the right of the net.

"Good try," called Kevin to Dennis as they skated toward the bench and the dressing room.

Dennis grinned. "Thanks."

The Cougars filed to their dressing room as Line Three came off the ice. Just as Thomas reached the bench, he heard someone yell, "Thomas!"

He turned and saw Claire in the stands. She had a bag of popcorn in one hand and a half-eaten hot dog in the other. She had the Transporter under one arm.

"There you are," she said. "I've been looking all over for you!"

"Well, I've been here the whole time," he explained, eyeing the half-eaten hot dog. "Where have you been?

Don't tell me you've been pigging out at the concession. Did you bring me anything?"

"A lady spilt her drink on my shoes and insisted she buy me these things," Claire said. "This is actually my second hot dog. I hope I can finish it."

Thomas' jaw dropped. "Well, tell her to come here and spill something on me. I'm starved!"

"Very funny."

Thomas looked intently at her. "Did you find a telephone?"

"Yeah. I tried phoning home again."

"What happened?"

"Same as last time. Our number is no longer in service."

"Why don't you try some other numbers?"

"I did. I tried four or five that I can remember."

"And?"

"Nothing."

"How about Auntie Barbara?"

"Same. They're all no longer in service," Claire said. "I think we should give up trying to phone anyone. But I do have some good news!"

"What?"

"While I was at the concession, I found the Transporter! It was sitting on the counter beside the popcorn machine." Claire held her bag of popcorn and hot dog in one hand, and with her free hand lifted the Transporter for Thomas to see. "I took it when no one was watching. We can go now! Maybe we'll go home this time. I'm ready to go home. How about you?"

Thomas was silent. "No. No, not now. We're in overtime. We can't go now."

"*What* are you talking about?" she said incredulously. "We can leave right now and no one would know the difference!"

"Well, I think I can help them. It's a tie game! *Sud-den death o-ver-time*," he said, emphasizing each syllable. He raised his eyebrows and looked at Claire closely to see if the words meant anything to her. They didn't.

"What if you lose?"

"What if we win?" countered Thomas. "If I were to leave now, I would always wonder what would've happened if I'd stayed. I couldn't possibly leave now."

"Thomas James!" exclaimed Claire, who only called him that when she was mad. "This whole thing is some kind of... illusion. It's not real. Sudden death overkill or not! I say we leave immediately!"

"It's sudden death *overtime*. Anyway, when we were in that registration place..."

"The Legislature," corrected Claire.

"Right. Anyway, when we were there, I wanted to leave and you wanted to stay. And we stayed, remember? It's my turn now."

"But this isn't real! It's all a weird dream, Thomas! I'm telling you, it's not real! Let's go, and now!"

Thomas kicked the ice gently with the toe of his skate. "Listen," he said. "This is the final game of the season. It's tied three-all and we're in sudden death. That's real enough for me!"

Claire frowned and took a bite of her hot dog. Thomas watched her lick the ketchup about to drip off the side of the bun.

"I... I gotta go," he said. "Come and find me when the game's over. We'll leave then."

In the dressing room, everyone talked at once. The coach paced the room, zipping and unzipping his leather jacket constantly. He ran his hands through the sparse hair on the sides of his head. After a few minutes, he spoke.

"Nice work, guys. I'm impressed beyond words. I knew you could do this and I know you can win this. You're outskating, outpassing, and outshooting these Movers. You can win this one. That last shot, Dennis, might have done it!"

Dennis stared at the blade of his stick, smiling.

"Dennis, if you get another chance..." The coach paused, a wide grin forming on his face. "...aim a *little* to the left." A few kids chuckled. "Now, let's go out there and win this one!"

The players jumped up and jammed toward the door. As they did, Dennis said, "Hey Thomas, thanks for setting me up. That was really cool. I've never had that kind of chance before."

"No problem," said Thomas. "If I can pass to you again, keep the blade of your stick sloped toward me. Then handle the puck until you get a good chance to shoot. And when you shoot, shoot where the goalie isn't."

"I will," promised Dennis.

Four minutes into the overtime period, the Movers almost scored. The first two Cougar lines were out of breath.

"Line Three, you're on," called the coach.

Kevin was doing up his skates, so the coach told Trevor, the boy already playing center, to stay on the ice. Unfortunately, when Kevin did come on, Trevor didn't come off in time and the Cougars got a penalty for having too many players on the ice. Kevin skated to the penalty box and Trevor back to the Cougar bench. Most of the Cougars on the bench were dumbfounded. They had been doing so well and now they were shorthanded! They knew they were in trouble.

Just before the faceoff, to the right of the Cougar goalie, Thomas skated over to his left defenseman.

"I'm going to try and get the puck back to you on the faceoff. When you get it, skate around behind our net and lob the puck down center ice." The defenseman nodded.

Then Thomas skated over to Dennis. "As soon as the puck is dropped, skate down right wing like lightning."

"But what if the Movers try—"

"It's now or never, Dennis. Just do it. Like lightning."

"Alright," agreed Dennis.

Thomas skated to the faceoff. The Mover forward stood a head taller than Thomas. Thomas pretended he was scared by looking around nervously, but as soon as the puck was dropped he lifted the Mover's stick and slapped the puck back to his defensemen. Then he raced down the ice. In a moment, the lobbed puck bounced in front of him and rolled toward the Mover blue line. Thomas saw Dennis skating wildly down right wing— arms, stick, and legs flying all over the place like an out of control cartoon character on a skateboard.

Thomas picked up the puck and stickhandled toward the goal. The Mover defenseman was coming at him hard and soon Thomas was too far to the left to take a good shot. He waited until the last possible moment, faked a slapshot, then made a quick pass over to Dennis, who perfectly cupped the puck with his stick and shot it into the net.

The referee blew his whistle, but it couldn't be heard over the roar of the crowd. The Cougars had won the game!

The whole Cougar team came off the bench and skated over to Dennis, dropping sticks and gloves on the way. Two of the bigger players picked him up and carried him on their shoulders. The crowd threw their hats into the air. The celebration was deafening. Even the Mover fans were clapping.

Thomas joined the backslapping procession around the ice. Then he saw Claire at the Cougar bench, smiling. He smiled back, turned, and looked over at Dennis who was waving madly at the crowd. Thomas waved to him and held up his thumb in congratulations. Dennis did the same.

Thomas skated to Claire.

"Nice pass, Thomas. So can we leave now or do you need to sign autographs first?" she said, grinning.

"We can leave now."

"What about your skates? Aren't you going to take them off?"

Thomas thought for a moment. "Well, I didn't have them on before we came here, so I probably won't have them on wherever we go."

"Do you think we'll finally be going home?"

"Well, we have to go home eventually, right? Now would be a good time. That's if it's still lunchtime at home. I know you've already eaten a couple of hot dogs, but I'm hungry. Do you think it's still lunchtime at home?"

Claire shrugged and handed Thomas the Transporter. She put her hand on his shoulder and he pushed the Activator.

There was a faint, high-pitched siren sound. Both Claire and Thomas felt dizzy as they began a slow motion head-over-heels somersault. The sound of the cheering crowd faded as the air rushed past them, quietly.

They both started to hear accordion music. It sounded like some kind of sad folk song.

Claire landed beside a rack of hanging pots and pans. As she landed, she bumped a tray of cutlery, which crashed to the floor. Several people in white aprons and hats turned to see what had happened.

One of them, a large man with food stains on his apron, frowned at her.

"Claire, try to be more careful!" he scolded.

Claire smiled weakly. Thomas was nowhere to be seen.

Discussion Questions

Describe Kevin and Dennis.

What did Thomas try to do to help Line Three?

When Claire found Thomas, she wanted to leave immediately. What were her reasons? What were Thomas' reasons for staying?

What should you do if you don't agree with other people's reasons or logic?

At the end of the chapter, Thomas and Claire were transported to a new location. Where do you think they are now?

chapter 8

Claire took a deep breath.

"I'm sorry," she apologized, looking around for Thomas.

"Don't worry about it," said the large man. "Just put the cutlery in the sink, then start dishing that Caesar salad into serving bowls." He pointed to a huge container of green salad.

Claire picked up the cutlery and set it in the nearby stainless steel sink before washing her hands. She wore a white apron and small white hat, just like everyone else in the kitchen. The aroma of baking lasagne filled the air as she spooned Caesar salad into the serving bowls. Claire thought it wouldn't be long before Thomas showed up.

Meanwhile, Thomas had landed on a French Provincial sofa, sprawled over the cushions. A plump lady in a light pink nursing uniform turned and shook her finger at him. Her auburn hair was in a bun and her face was red.

"Please do not jump on the furniture!" she scolded.

"I'm sorry," he said as he stood. That's when he noticed the light blue smock covering his clothes. He was surprised to see his name on a nametag, under the word "Volunteer."

He gazed through the large window beside him. On the other side was a dining room with about thirty small tables. Grey- and white-haired people sat around them. Many were in wheelchairs. Most were eating, or had people helping them eat.

"Now, if you're actually planning on helping with supper, please do so now," requested the woman. "The residents have already started."

"Yes, ma'am," said Thomas respectfully. He looked at the people in the dining room and scratched his head. "Excuse me, ma'am?"

"It's Mrs. Billings," she said, thumbing through some papers.

"Uh, Mrs. Billings, could you... uh... tell me how to pronounce the name of the resident I'm to help?"

Mrs. Billings peered over her glasses. "J-O-N-E-S. JONES," she enunciated clearly. She shook her head, picked up her papers, and stormed down the hallway.

Thomas stood still for a moment, then tucked in his shirt and tied his right shoelace.

Now all I have to do is find someone named Jones and figure out what I'm supposed to do when I find him—or her, he thought to himself as he walked into the room. The smell of lasagne and garlic bread filled the air. He took a deep breath. *I think I'm going to like this!*

Everyone had nametags, but he couldn't find anyone named Jones. He went over to a large black woman in a blue smock serving food to a table of grey-haired ladies in wheelchairs. Her nametag read "Angela."

"Excuse me, Angela. Do you know where Mr. Jones is?"

Angela put down a tray of food. She looked at Thomas quizzically, hands on her hips. "Do you mean Mr. Jones? Mr. Robert Jones?" She tilted her head toward Thomas. "Or Mrs. Peggy Jones?"

"Oh, yes, of course! That would be... Mrs. Peggy Jones," he guessed.

"Good. Mr. Jones is out with the shuttle bus right now."

"Well, do you know where Mrs. Jones is?"

Angela saw Thomas' nametag. "Thomas, if you're assigned to her this evening, you might be too late. Supper is almost over, honey." She frowned. "She usually sits over by the atrium. Take a look for her there."

"Thank you!" said Thomas, turning and walking away.

"Thomas," called Angela. "The atrium is that way." She pointed in the opposite direction.

"Right. Thanks."

Thomas walked past a number of tables and realized he was getting closer to the kitchen. He closed his eyes and breathed through his nose. The aroma of garlic bread was fabulous.

"Excuse me, son," said an elderly lady with thin grey hair and reading glasses hanging on a little chain around her neck. "Would you be so kind as to get me some lasagne?"

"Sure can," said Thomas helpfully, wondering if he could get some for himself while he was at it. He took a glance at the lady's nametag: she was Peggy Jones! "Oh, Mrs. Jones, I'm your helper today!"

She smiled. "Wonderful! You've arrived just in time."

Thomas walked over to the counter where several people served food. He picked up two plates and handed them to the server behind the counter. "This stuff is sure popular tonight," said the server, placing lasagne on each plate.

Thomas continued along the counter where Caesar salad was served. As he held out the plates, he heard someone exclaim, "Thomas!"

He gasped when he saw Claire holding a serving spoon full of Caesar salad.

"What are *you* doing here?" he whispered.

"I'm serving Caesar salad. What are you doing *here*?"

"I'm on my way to Mrs. Jones with this plate of lasagne."

"Let me guess. You're getting two plates in case someone else wants some?"

"Very funny. I just thought, you know, that I might have some myself while I'm at it."

"The lady in charge of the kitchen told us we could eat after everyone else. That probably applies to you, too."

Thomas could smell the lasagne on his plate. The cheese was bubbling on the edges and the aroma gently wafted toward him.

"Right." He looked at Claire. "Anyway, have you seen the Transporter or anything?"

"No, I haven't."

"Well, keep your eyes peeled," Thomas instructed, looking from side to side and crouching a little, like he didn't want anyone to hear. He lowered his voice. "I'm going to deliver this food. I'll find you later." He turned to leave, hesitated, then whispered. "Oh, Claire. One other thing."

Claire bent down a little. "Yes? What is it?"

Thomas looked around quickly, then leaned toward her. "Where's the garlic bread?"

Claire sighed. "Over on that table," she said, pointing with her serving spoon.

A minute later, Thomas set one of the plates in front of Mrs. Jones.

"Sorry, I got some salad and garlic bread for you by mistake. I know you only wanted lasagne," he explained.

"That's fine. Say, why don't you tell me your name?"

"I'm Thomas. Thomas Brampton."

"Pleased to meet you, Thomas," Mrs. Jones said, holding out a trembling hand.

Thomas shook her hand, then sat down and began to eat his meal.

"What have you been up to today?" she asked, biting into a small mouthful of lasagne.

"Oh, just, uh... you know, hanging around. How about you?"

"Oh, it's been a lovely day. This morning, I read an article about geraniums. Then I sat outside after lunch and enjoyed the afternoon sun. It was just beautiful. After that, I came inside for a nap. Pretty soon it was suppertime. The day has just flown by."

Thomas nodded as he ate his lasagne and salad.

Mrs. Jones took another small mouthful. "Would you like my garlic bread?" she asked, noticing Thomas' garlic bread had already disappeared.

"Yeah, sure. I mean, uh, yes, please."

As Thomas finished his meal and scraped the plate clean, he noticed Mrs. Jones staring at him.

"You were hungry, weren't you?" she said. "It sure is good, isn't it? If you can believe it, my husband used to make lasagne like this. You would have enjoyed it, too. He made the best lasagne in the world! Lasagne and quiche were his specialties. They were delicious." Mrs. Jones stared across the room for awhile. She put her napkin on the table and looked at Thomas. "My mother was a good cook, too. I remember the hamburger soup she made when I was growing up."

Thomas wiped his face with his sleeve. He scratched his ear. "So, where did you grow up?"

* * *

Claire finished the last of her lasagne and wiped her face with a napkin.

"You may go help your resident now," instructed her supervisor, handing her a light blue smock.

"Could you remind me of their name?" asked Claire as she hung up her apron and hat and put on the smock, "and how I may help them today?"

"Certainly. It's Edwards. Mr. Francis Edwards. Just down the hall past the library. He often likes the newspaper read to him."

Claire walked out of the dining room and into the hallway. She saw a "Library" sign above a door.

Good, she thought. *I'm heading in the right direction.* She walked past the library, reading the names beside each door as she went along. *Pauls. Asselstine. Wong. Edwards.* She stopped, then said to herself, *Well, this is the guy.*

She tidied her hair, opened the door, and walked in. An old man with thick glasses sat in a rocking chair. Mr. Edwards was asleep, his head flopped to one side and his mouth open. He snored loudly, especially when he inhaled. He wore a striped tie and cardigan. Something was spilt on his sweater, like pudding, and it had dried in a long drip.

Mr. Edwards made a sharp snort, opened his eyes, and straightened in his chair. He swallowed, then looked at Claire for a moment.

"Oh," he said. "Is it time for my chess game? And what is your name, young lady?"

"It's Claire, Mr. Edwards."

"Claire. Very good. And you know my name already. Good for you. Well, the chess set is over in that cupboard."

Chess! Claire thought as she walked to the cupboard. *I haven't played chess for... forever!*

She placed the chess board on a table by Mr. Edwards.

"Do you want to be black or white?" he asked.

"Oh... I'll be black, I guess."

Claire set up the chess pieces.

Mr. Edwards said, "E2 to E4 please."

Claire stared at the old gentleman for a moment. "What did you say?"

"King's pawn E2 to E4."

Claire vaguely recalled her dad teaching her about chess moves two or three years earlier. Mr. Edwards pointed at the chess board, his hand shaking terribly.

"I can't move the men very easily," he said. "Move my king's pawn forward two spaces, please."

"Right," understood Claire. Suddenly the chess language came to her. She moved Mr. Edwards' pawn.

"Thank you," he said.

Claire moved one of her pawns, then Mr. Edwards said, "Knight G1 to H3." Claire moved Mr. Edwards' knight. Then she moved her own queen.

"Trying to set up an early defence, I see," he observed. "Maybe I should do the same. Queen's pawn D2 to D4."

The game progressed steadily until Mr. Edwards took a long time to decide his next move. Claire looked around the room. One wall was covered with framed pictures. There were black-and-white pictures of a baby, a boy in overalls, and a young man with an old-fashioned bicycle. There was a picture of someone in a uniform standing beside an airplane. There was a picture of a man getting an award. There was a wedding picture, then a picture of a young man holding a baby with his wife beside him. Then a picture with two children. The pictures eventually continued in colour, with the children later in life, getting bigger. There were graduation pictures, then more wedding pictures.

"Who are all the people in these pictures?" asked Claire.

Mr. Edwards raised his arm and pointed a shaking finger to the far end. "Those are me when I was little. That's my wife." He smiled, pointing to a black-and-white picture of a beautiful woman beside a young man with a black moustache. "I had a moustache back then. And those are our kids, Joseph and Elizabeth." His hand shook almost uncontrollably as he pointed at each picture. "That's when they graduated from college. Joseph is a dentist and Elizabeth is a math teacher. There they are with their spouses, and kids."

Mr. Edwards put his arm down and took a breath. He continued to describe his grandchildren, where they lived, what they were doing, what they were like. Then he described his four great grandchildren. When he finished, he turned toward Claire, his eyes sparkling.

"Best thing I ever did was marry Olive. She was a princess," he said, staring at her picture. "I've had a good life, you know. A good life."

Claire began to see the resemblance between Mr. Edwards and the pictures of when he was younger.

She cleared her throat. "May I ask how old you are, Mr. Edwards?"

"Sure!" he exclaimed with a smile. "I'm ninety-one. Isn't that something?" He thought for a moment. "Say, what about our chess game? Whose move is it anyway?"

"I think it's yours."

"Oh. Right." He studied the board for a moment. "Queen D1 to F3."

Claire moved the queen. Then she moved her own knight. "Mr. Edwards, what's it like being ninety-one?"

Mr. Edwards grinned. "Well, how old are you, Claire?"

"Thirteen. I'll be fourteen next month."

"Thirteen! I remember when I was thirteen. You probably wonder if that was actually possible, but I clearly remember being thirteen. It doesn't seem that long ago, either." He looked off into the distance. "Goes by quickly."

"What does?"

"Life. It goes by quickly. It sometimes doesn't seem like it, but it sure does. I can remember when I was thirteen, and now here I am, ninety-one. How did that happen so fast?" A thoughtful smile spread across his face as his eyes returned to the chess board. "Knight B1 to C3."

The chess game continued for several minutes without conversation. Then Claire asked, "Is that you in the picture beside the airplane?"

Mr. Edwards looked at the picture but didn't say anything. He looked at it for a long time. "Yes, it is."

"Can you tell me about the medals on your uniform?"

Mr. Edwards hesitated. "I was a navigator on a Wellington Bomber in World War II. While returning to the air base one night, we were shot down over France. Before the plane crashed, I freed the gunner who was jammed in his turret. We both got out in just enough time for our parachutes to open."

"So you saved his life?"

Mr. Edwards slowly nodded. "Yes... Yes, I guess so."

"Well, that's great," blurted Claire excitedly. "That's wonderful!"

Mr. Edwards spoke slowly. "Three of the crew got out in time. Two never made it. One of them was a very good friend. We enlisted together."

There was a long pause. Mr. Edwards sniffed. "Did you move yet, Claire?"

"Yes, I did. My bishop," she said. "Check."

Mr. Edwards looked at the chess board, his eyes glassy.

"Can you tell me about that picture of you and the pretty lady?"

Almost instantly, his face brightened. "That's Olive. She was my wife. Died nine years and... three months ago. She was a gem."

"How long were you married?" she inquired.

"Almost sixty years. I don't think I realized how good it was being married to her. I wish..." Mr. Edwards stared at the picture, wiping away a tear.

"How about this one?" she asked, pointing to a picture of Mr. Edwards shaking the hand of a man wearing a tuxedo.

"Oh, that one's kind of embarrassing," he admitted.

Claire waited for Mr. Edwards to talk, a small grin forming on her face.

"I was nominated for an award," he said with a chuckle. "I must have been the only person nominated, so they had to give it to me."

Claire walked over to the picture. The man in the tuxedo held a plaque that said "Citizen of the Year 1974."

"Wow, you were the citizen of the year in 1974? That's awesome!"

Just then, Thomas came into the room with a tray. "I've brought some oatmeal raisin cookies," he announced.

"Well, how did you know those are my favourite?" asked Mr. Edwards.

"Thomas, how did you know I was here?" asked Claire.

"I see you two know each other," observed Mr. Edwards. "No introductions necessary, except for me. I'm Mr. Edwards."

Thomas put the plate of cookies on the night table and shook Mr. Edwards' hand. "Nice to meet you, Mr. Edwards. I'm Thomas. Who's winning the chess game?"

Mr. Edwards grinned. "Well, I think Claire is, but it's my move, so she'd better watch out."

"Mr. Edwards was telling me about the pictures on the wall," explained Claire.

"Sure are a lot of them," Thomas said. "Who are all those people in that picture?" He pointed to a gold-framed colour photo of a dozen people standing in a flower garden.

"Oh, that's my kids and their spouses and my grandchildren and two of my great-grandchildren. They're a great bunch."

"Where do they live?" asked Thomas.

Mr. Edwards thought for a moment. "East coast. I don't see them very often. Last time was two years ago, but they send me pictures from time to time. Here's one." He pointed to a curled photograph on his night table. The boy in the picture looked quite a bit older than the photograph on the wall.

"Hey, is that the Eiffel Tower?" Thomas walked over to a small black-and-white picture on the wall.

"Yes, it is," said Mr. Edwards.

"That's in France, isn't it?" asked Thomas.

"Yes, it's in Paris."

Thomas had a smug look on his face.

"My wife and I went on a trip there once," continued Mr. Edwards. "It was marvellous. We saw the Place de la Concorde, the Arc de Triomphe, and spent a whole day just wandering around the Louvre!"

"What's a loo-vra?" asked Thomas.

"It's the most incredible art gallery you've ever seen. The statues and paintings are absolutely amazing. You can just sit and look at some of them for ages. We had such fun." Mr. Edwards began to talk faster. "There was a photographer for a French newspaper who took our picture while we were at the Louvre and we ended up on the front page the next day! It was so much fun. Oh! I almost forgot! While we were going up the elevator in the Eiffel Tower, it stopped halfway. We were stuck in there for over an hour with a Polish lady and a couple from Amsterdam. We couldn't communicate, but we had a big lunch basket with us so we had a picnic right there in the elevator, checkered tablecloth and all! We laughed so hard we had tears running down our faces. Olive and I had such a good time! Such a good time."

A male nurse came into the room. "Time for your medications, Mr. Edwards. I see you have some visitors. How's the chess game going?"

"Fine, just fine, thank you, Marty," replied Mr. Edwards as he swallowed one of three pills with the glass of water Marty held for him.

Thomas took the opportunity to whisper in Claire's ear. "I found the Transporter. It was in the laundry room. I hid it under some pillowcases."

"Does that mean we should leave?" asked Claire reluctantly.

"I guess so, but... could we stay just a bit longer? I never thought I would enjoy hanging out in a place like this, but I had a great talk with this little old lady named Mrs. Jones. She used to be a WREN in the Second World War!"

"A what?" asked Claire.

"She was in the Navy. I'll tell you more about it later. After the war, she and her husband homesteaded in the Peace River area. They lived in a log house without running water or electricity. It was hard to believe." Thomas paused and rubbed his chin. "She was really cool to talk with."

"Thank you, Marty," called Mr. Edwards as the nurse left his room. "So now, Claire, whose move is it?"

"Yours, I think, Mr. Edwards."

"Alright then," he said. "Bishop F1 to B5. Check."

"I'm in trouble now!" Claire admitted. She rested her chin in her hands as her eyes darted back and forth across the chessboard. She lifted her head and chuckled. "I think its checkmate, Mr. Edwards. You win! Congratulations! How'd that happen?"

Mr. Edwards sat back in his chair and smiled. "Thank you, Claire. Would you please put the chess game away for me?"

"Certainly."

"And while you're doing so, tell me what you two like to do in your spare time," he inquired.

"Well, Thomas likes to make things," answered Claire.

"Yeah, and play computer games," interjected Thomas. "There's this really cool one called *Galaxy Rangers* where you blow up the enemy space fleet with..." He stopped talking when he saw the puzzled look on Mr. Edwards' face. "Anyway, it's really cool."

"What's a computer game?" asked Mr. Edwards.

"It's like watching TV, except you make stuff happen."

"I've watched a lot of TV over the years, but now wish I hadn't."

"Why not?" asked Claire.

"Well, watching some TV is okay. There's some good programs on, from time to time. But those hours... maybe hundreds of hours... sitting there, staring, not doing anything productive, they're all gone, forever. I wished I'd used my time better. You know, reading, helping people, spending more time with..." Mr. Edwards gazed at the photos on the wall. He cleared his throat. "It's funny. My eyes aren't good enough to read anymore, but I can still watch TV. I'd rather read, but... now I can't." He sighed, then turned to Claire. "And what kind of things do you like doing?"

"Oh, I love to read."

"Perhaps you'd be willing to read to me the next time you come and visit."

"That would be fun," agreed Claire, not exactly sure how to answer.

Another nurse came into the room. "Time to get ready for bed, Mr. Edwards," she said.

"Thank you, Helen. Well, Thomas and Claire, thank you for coming. I hope you can come again soon. See you next time."

"Thank you, Mr. Edwards," Thomas and Claire chimed as they left the room. "Goodbye."

They walked down the hall to the laundry room and closed the door. The room smelled like laundry detergent and folded sheets. Thomas found the Transporter.

Claire noticed Thomas looking at his shoes. "What's the matter?"

"I dunno. I guess I feel kind of sad for Mrs. Jones. Her family doesn't come and see her very often and she's stuck in this place and everything."

"Mr. Edwards' family doesn't visit here very often, either," said Claire. "But don't you think this place is kinda nice?"

Thomas nodded. "Yes, that's true." He was quiet for a moment. "I never really thought that old people were, you know, so interesting. Or that they were young, like us, once."

"I know what you mean."

"But they just seem... lonely. I hope we can come back again sometime. Somehow."

"That isn't likely. But if we ever make it home, maybe we could visit the people at that seniors lodge just down the street from us."

Thomas' face brightened. "Great idea, Claire! Great idea. Maybe the Transporter will take us home so we can do that right now!"

"I hope so." Claire suddenly became serious. "Thomas... what if it doesn't? And instead of a nice place like this, what if we end up somewhere we don't want to be—someplace... dangerous?"

Thomas studied the Transporter as he turned it around in his hands. "I don't know what else we can do." He paused and put his hand on her arm. "Don't worry, Claire. We'll figure it out."

Claire put her hand on Thomas' shoulder as he pushed the Activator.

The lights in the laundry room dimmed as they began their head-over-heels spinning. The air rushed by slowly. The smell of laundry detergent faded. At first, they only heard the sound of a high-pitched siren.

Then they heard running water. A lot of water. Eventually it sounded like a roaring river. A moment later, Thomas and Claire were soaked with spray.

Discussion Questions

What do Thomas and Claire do when they find out they are to spend time with someone at the seniors lodge?

What surprised Thomas and Claire about the seniors they visited?

If you were living in a seniors home, what would be important for you?

At the end of the chapter, Thomas and Claire were transported to a new location. Where do you think they are now?

Thomas

Claire

Thomas and Claire landed in an open canoe, Thomas on the stern seat and Claire between the bow seat and bow deck. Her eyes were wide open. Less than one hundred meters away, she saw the biggest wave she had ever seen.

"Thomas!" she shouted. "We're going to be swamped!"

The canoe wasn't on a lake or gentle creek; it was in the middle of boiling rapids on a raging river. Foaming waves broke over the bow. Claire's mouth went dry as she saw how quickly the towering wave approached. She turned toward Thomas, grateful he was there, but shocked when she realized he had no paddle. They both saw the paddles in the bottom of the canoe. Two paddles, two lifejackets, and two backpacks. None of the gear was tied down.

"Quick, Claire! Grab a paddle and start back-paddling!" yelled Thomas.

Claire reached behind her to get a paddle. "Maybe we should put on these lifejackets first, in case we sink!"

This was a good suggestion as the canoe hammered wave after wave and water splashed in continuously. The backpacks and life jackets began to float around in the bottom of the canoe.

"No, not now!" yelled Thomas, already paddling. "Let's get under control, then put on the lifejackets."

Thomas could also see what was coming and it didn't look good. Crashing haystack waves threatened to sink the canoe, but they were nothing compared to the looming monster wave.

They both back-paddled as hard as they could, trying to slow the canoe down so it wouldn't smash so hard into the waves and take on water.

"Hey!" shouted Claire. "There's some quiet water over there. Let's head toward it!"

Thomas looked where Claire had pointed. He couldn't see anything except an ocean of foaming waves. Then he saw it—a small, calm backwater behind some jagged boulders.

"Good idea!" he yelled enthusiastically.

They paddled furiously but made little progress toward the calm water. They knew how to paddle a canoe, having gone on canoe trips with their parents. Now they were on their own and wished they had paid more attention.

The canoe hit the gigantic wave. The water cascaded over the bow and knocked Claire off her seat and into the river. She lost her paddle and desperately lunged for a lifejacket as the canoe flipped over and sank.

"Claire!" yelled Thomas as he hit the water. "Grab a—"

Thomas vanished into the foam.

The cold water was paralyzing. Thomas came to the surface, struggled for breath, and saw a backpack in front of him. He reached for it, grabbed hold, then disappeared again under the frothy waves.

Claire got to shore first. As soon as the water was shallow enough that her hands could touch the rocks on the bottom, she stood up and stumbled to the riverbank. She shivered uncontrollably and dropped the lifejacket on the rocky shore. She searched the rapids downstream, looking for Thomas. She didn't see anything, not even the canoe.

"Thomas! Thom–mas! Thommmm–mas!" she called. She heard nothing except the roar of the rapids.

The sun shone brightly in a blue sky. Claire would have happily soaked up its warmth, but all she could think of was Thomas. She staggered a few steps upstream, stopped, and shook her head.

Think! Think!

She took a few more halting steps, then decided that Thomas had most likely been washed downstream by the current.

She walked almost three hundred meters before she saw him. There he was, lying on a massive tree trunk jammed on a shoal about ten meters from shore. The river raced past him.

"Thomas! Are you alright?"

Thomas lifted his head and nodded sluggishly. He pulled himself up onto the tree trunk. The water was knee-deep on the shoal. Holding his backpack in one hand, and using his paddle as a walking stick, he waded through the frigid water toward Claire. The fast water gradually went from his knees to his waist. He slogged along, hoping it wouldn't get any deeper. He almost lost his balance twice, but finally reached the shore and collapsed in front of Claire.

She helped him sit up and wrapped her arms around him. They both shivered.

"We need to get warm, and fast," she stammered. "Maybe there are some... matches in your backpack."

She fumbled with the zipper and finally got the pack open. There was a book of matches in a waterproof container and several other items, but she left them in the backpack and dropped it to the ground.

"Come on, let's get a fire going," she encouraged him as she got up and walked toward the spruce trees along the shore. Thomas grimaced and slowly got to his feet. He walked like Frankenstein, his legs stiff with cold.

They broke several dead branches off the trees nearby, knowing spruce would light easily and burn hot, and piled them on a sandy part of the shore. As they collected the wood, they realized they were on an island in the river. The channel on the other side of the island was wider than the channel they had just come through.

Claire's hands shook as she tried to light a match. It went out. Thomas was too cold to even try.

"D... d... don't worry, y... y... you'll do it this t... t... time," he sputtered.

Claire struck a second match but couldn't hold it still. It went out.

"Here," said Thomas, "I'll hold s... s... some of these b... b... branches and you put a lit m... match under them."

He picked some of the finest twigs from the branches and held them tightly in his shaking hand. Claire lit a third match and held the tiny flame under the twigs. They started to smoke, then burn—a small flame at first, then larger. Thomas carefully placed the bundle of burning twigs on the ground. They both added more twigs until the flame was strong enough to handle bigger pieces.

They warmed themselves by the fire for some time before Thomas spoke.

"Well, we're in a real pickle," he announced, shivering occasionally. He threw a branch on the fire. "I thought we might be heading home from that seniors place, but here we are stranded on an island in the middle of a river somewhere, surrounded by rapids. We have no

Transporter, no canoe, no warm clothes, only one paddle, and one lifejacket. Reminds me of that camping trip we went on with Mom and Dad when we forgot to pack all the kitchen stuff and sleeping bags."

"But we do have a nice warm fire. And a backpack," Claire said, rubbing her hands near the flames. "Say, let's see what else is inside this backpack." She opened it and pulled out a pot with a wire loop handle and a package of chicken noodle soup. "Hey, this will be great!"

She walked to the river, scooped some water into the pot, then returned and set it in the fire to boil.

"Wait," said Thomas. "Let's get the fire going a little more first. It's too small to boil water."

"No, it's fine," disagreed Claire, adding sticks around the pot. "It'll boil quickly, then we'll add the soup." She read the instructions on the soup package. "Wait. It says to add contents to cold water, then heat to a boil."

"I'll take it out," sighed Thomas in an oh-brother tone of voice. He found a stick, hooked it under the wire handle of the pot, and began to lift it out of the fire. The stick snapped and the pot fell, dumping its contents and dousing the flames.

"Thomas James!" gasped Claire. "How could you do something so stupid?!"

"Me! You're the one who didn't bother reading the soup instructions!"

"Well, we wouldn't have needed a fire in the first place if you had kept us upright in that stupid canoe!"

"Me? Me? We wouldn't have needed this fire if you had done more than scream at every wave!" yelled Thomas.

"Well, we wouldn't even be here if you hadn't built that stupid Transporter."

"Well, we *are* here. But we might be upright in a canoe somewhere if you had used your paddle at all, and now you've lost the stupid thing."

Claire frowned and turned away. Then she smiled, slightly. "Now I know what it means to be up the creek without a paddle."

"Very funny."

There was a long silence.

Claire sighed. "I don't like it when we argue."

Thomas stood silently, then walked over to a nearby spruce tree and collected more branches.

They eventually got the fire going again and boiled more water, this time with the soup mix in the water first. They emptied the backpack and found a survival blanket that looked like a large sheet of aluminum foil, a pocketknife, a small container of hot chocolate, and two plastic mugs. They poured the soup into the mugs and took a drink.

"This soup reminds me of Mom," said Thomas, taking a sip. Claire nodded.

When they finished the soup, they rinsed out the pot and made hot chocolate. Their clothes took a long time to dry and they had to turn themselves regularly to dry all sides.

"We better gather a bunch of wood before it gets dark," suggested Thomas, "It could be a long night."

They collected a good pile of firewood, including some logs that had washed up along the shore. Together they made a log and branch lean-to near the fire. Claire tucked the survival blanket inside it, making a kind of open-faced tent. The lean-to was just big enough for one person and was like a warm oven inside, the foil blanket reflecting heat from the fire.

They decided to take turns sleeping, the other keeping the fire going throughout the night. Claire would sleep first. As she made herself comfortable inside the lean-to, she pondered Thomas' earlier comments about their situation.

"We've been though some pretty challenging things so far, but this does seem the most hopeless," she said, the firelight reflecting off their faces.

"What do you mean?"

"Well, like, how will we ever be able to get off this island without the Transporter or the canoe, and with the water so freezing cold?"

Thomas shrugged. "Maybe we'll find the Transporter and get out of here. Or maybe we'll find the canoe. It has to wash up somewhere. Maybe it washed up further down this island. Let's check it out in the morning."

Claire gazed at the stars appearing in the night sky. "Let's say we find the Transporter before the canoe. What if we keep going from place to place and never get home?"

Thomas shrugged. He picked up a large stick with a wide end and began whittling it with the pocketknife.

"Whatever are you doing now?" asked Claire.

"Making a canoe paddle, what else?"

* * *

Claire woke in the middle of the night and saw Thomas asleep beside the glowing embers of the fire. Feeling chilled, she put more wood on the fire.

"Thomas. Thomas! Your turn for the lean-to."

Thomas opened his eyes slowly, crawled over to the lean-to, lay down, and fell asleep in one motion. Claire noticed the paddle Thomas had carved. She picked it up and chuckled. It actually resembled a paddle, even though the shaft was quite thick. The blade had the right shape, although it was thick, too.

As she sat by the crackling fire, watching sparks spiral into the dark sky, she wondered what was happening at home and if her parents were worried.

She picked up the pocketknife Thomas had left on the ground and started whittling away on the paddle.

* * *

By morning, Claire had fallen asleep by the fire. They both woke about the same time.

Something was wrong. Something sounded different.

Thomas noticed it first. He got up and walked around, trying to figure out what it was. He made his way toward the river and guessed what had changed before he got there. The water had gone down—by almost half a meter! The huge rapids were now medium-sized. The shore extended five meters further from where it had been the night before.

Thomas peered far downriver and saw something purple along the shore.

What's that? he wondered as he walked toward it.

Eventually he saw it was a backpack and ran to pick it up. It was soaking wet and muddy, but still zipped up. He ran back to Claire, who was stirring the coals of the fire.

"Hey Claire, guess what I found?" exclaimed Thomas, holding up the backpack for her to see.

Her jaw dropped. "Good for you, Thomas! Quick! Open it up!"

In a moment, they found packages of instant oatmeal, two soggy boxes of raisins, some fishing line... and the Transporter.

"Yahoo!" yelled Claire when she saw the Transporter. "Now we can leave!"

"How about some oatmeal first?" suggested Thomas hungrily.

"What? No! We might end up at home, and if we do we can eat all we want there."

"Claire, let's eat first," pleaded Thomas. "If for some reason we don't go home, who knows if we'll have anything to eat where we do end up. But we do have something to eat right now! This could be our last meal for a while.

Let's take a vote." Thomas raised his right hand. "All in favour of eating breakfast before we leave, say 'aye.'"

"Alright, alright!" Claire sighed, pushing her straggly hair over her shoulders. "But you can have my raisins. I hate raisins. I'm not anywhere near hungry enough to eat raisins! I'll get some water in the pot, but we leave as soon as we finish eating, okay?"

"Okay," agreed Thomas.

The oatmeal was delicious. Thomas thought it especially so because he got a double portion of raisins.

When Claire finished eating, she picked up the pot to wash it out.

"Don't bother," said Thomas. "Just leave it here. We can't take it with us."

"Why not?" asked Claire.

"Well, I didn't have skates on when we landed at that seniors place. Doesn't matter what we have on or have with us. We end up with whatever we end up with."

Claire put the pot down and handed Thomas the Transporter. She put her hand on his shoulder. "Let's go."

Thomas pushed the Activator. Nothing happened.

"Not this again," he groaned.

He banged it against the side of his leg, then pushed the Activator again. He tried everything he could think of and finally shook his head in disgust.

"Maybe it doesn't work because it got wet," wondered Claire.

Thomas took out the two double-A batteries. The battery compartment was full of water.

"I bet they shorted out," he said.

"What does that mean?"

"It means we aren't going anywhere until..."

"Until what?"

"Until we get some different batteries."

They sat quietly for a few moments.

"Let's walk around this island and see what we can find," Claire suggested.

"Like what?"

"Like batteries."

"Oh, right! They'll be in little waterproof packages. Uh, let me guess... oh, I know, they'll be sitting underneath a *current* bush."

Claire frowned. "Oh, come on! Let's look around. What else are we going to do?" She started walking along the shore. "Current bush! Oh brother!"

They walked about a kilometer downstream, to the very tip of the island. When they got there, they found a calm backwater with logs floating in a circular motion. The logs were unaffected by the fast water of the converging channels zipping past nearby.

One log had no bark on it and seemed very smooth. Claire watched it for a while, then exclaimed, "Thomas! That's our canoe! It's upside down!"

"Yesssss!" cheered Thomas. "You're right!"

The keel of the canoe could be seen just above the water, an air pocket underneath keeping it afloat. The canoe drifted around in a large circle with logs and other debris.

"How are we going to get it?" asked Claire. "I'm not going in that freezing water again!"

Thomas sat down on a boulder and scrunched up his nose. His dad had once told him that a submerged canoe weighed hundreds of kilograms. He didn't want to wade out into the ice-cold water to get it, plus it was probably way over his head. He knew he might not have much choice in the matter.

He studied the canoe as it gently floated around. Then he noticed what looked like a long snake on the downstream side. It was the painter, a long rope tied to one end of the canoe.

Suddenly, he got up and began to run back to the campsite.

"Where are you going, Thomas?" called Claire. "What are you doing?"

"Wait here!" he yelled. "I'll be right back!"

About fifteen minutes later, Thomas returned out of breath. He had the cooking pot and fishing line. He held up the line for Claire to see.

She eyed it suspiciously. "What are you going to do with that?"

"Watch," answered Thomas, panting. He tied a rock to one end of the fishing line and unwound the rest along the shore. Then he gave the other end to Claire. "Wrap this end around your hand and don't let go." Claire held onto the line and sat down.

He picked up the end with the rock and threw it toward the canoe. It landed about three meters short. He pulled in the line and tried again. This time, the rock hit the canoe. Claire rose to her feet.

Thomas pulled the line in and threw the rock a third time. It landed in the water on the other side of the painter. As he carefully pulled the line in, it got caught on the painter, which slowly moved toward Thomas.

"Thomas, you're brilliant!" Claire cheered, watching the painter move closer and closer to the shore.

When the painter was close enough, Thomas reached into the water and took hold of it. He smiled. "Would you wind up this fishing line, please?" he asked politely. "Then come and help me with this canoe."

Claire wound up the line and put it by a big rock. "What are we going to do now?"

"We'll pull the canoe to the shore, dump out the water, then make plans."

Pulling in the canoe was harder work than they

thought. Their dad had been right; it did weigh hundreds of kilograms.

"Now what?" Claire asked when the canoe was close to shore.

"Well, we have to get one end up out of the water. Remember last summer when Dad and I tipped in the Brierlie Rapids? The canoe was upside down when we got it to shore so Dad lifted one end. Then we were able to flip it over. At least, I think that's what he did. Let's try."

They waded into the water. It seemed colder than the day before and their feet quickly became numb. They lifted the canoe with all their might, but couldn't get one end out of the water enough to flip it.

"Let's try rolling it over," said Claire. That was easier to do, but when the canoe rolled upright, it stayed full of water.

"Let's bail the water with the pot," suggested Thomas.

They took turns bailing, but water lapped back into the end of the canoe furthest from shore almost as fast as they bailed it out.

"Here, you bail," directed Claire, "I'll use my hands."

They made a little more progress, then Thomas went onto the shore and pulled the canoe with all his might. It hardly moved. They bailed more. Thomas pulled again. Nothing.

"We've got to keep trying," he said.

After a long time bailing, Thomas pulled on the canoe and it moved a few centimeters. He was encouraged. More bailing, more pulling. Slowly they moved the canoe high enough onto the shore that they could dump out the remaining water.

Thomas sat on a rock and wiped the sweat off his forehead. "I think we should take the canoe downstream and look for stuff. Maybe we'll find some batteries. If we flipped in the river and lost stuff from our canoe, maybe other people have, too. There could be a goldmine of stuff around here."

Claire folded her arms. "Are you kidding? You teased me this morning about looking for batteries. Do you really think we'll find two double-A batteries anywhere? Even if we happened to find any, do you suppose they'd work? And besides," she added, waving one arm downstream, "we don't know what it's like further downriver. There might be worse rapids than what we went through yesterday, and I don't want to do that again!"

Thomas scratched his armpit and squinted one eye shut. "Okay then. What's your plan?"

Claire puckered her lips and rubbed her chin. "Well, uh... I..." She walked around, then crossed her arms again. "If you're right about other people losing stuff, let's take a look around this island first. Then let's head downstream."

* * *

The search around the island resulted in a rusty tin, a pair of broken sunglasses, and a short piece of rope. Back at their campsite, Thomas and Claire gathered their few belongings and made sure the fire was out.

"Hey, you did an awesome job on this paddle, Claire!" exclaimed Thomas, admiring the carved paddle as they walked to the canoe.

"Well, you started it. I just made it a little lighter."

When they got to the canoe, Thomas tied the backpacks to the thwart—a brace holding the sides of the canoe together. He began to put on the lifejacket when Claire stopped him.

"I think I should wear the lifejacket," she suggested.

149

"Why? I'm younger than you."

"Yes, but I'm a girl."

"What's that got to do with anything? Besides, if we tip again, I don't want to sink like I did last time."

"Neither do I. But you shouldn't have to worry. You're a better swimmer than me."

"That's not necessarily true."

She glared at him. "You're a better swimmer than me and you know it. You have your level eight. That's further than I went."

"Yes, but I just barely passed."

"That's funny. Last month I heard you boasting to Brian McCullough that you were at the top of your swimming class, and now you say you just barely passed. You're the biggest manipulator in the world!"

There was a long pause. "Okay, you wear the lifejacket." He handed it over, then turned and wistfully looked upstream. "See how you feel when I drown."

Claire rolled her eyes. "Okay. Let's take turns. You wear it for fifteen minutes. After that—"

"Then I'll wear it for fifteen minutes!" said Thomas.

"No, then I'll wear it!"

"Alright." Thomas took the lifejacket and put it on. "You sit in the bow and I'll sit in the stern."

Claire frowned. "What? Wait a minute. If you're in the stern, I should get the lifejacket."

"Whatever for?"

Claire put her hands on her hips. "Well, the person in the stern decides where we go and steers and calls the shots. If the person in the stern makes a bad decision, the person in the bow suffers. Therefore, the person in the bow should get the lifejacket. What'll it be? The bow with the lifejacket, or the stern without?"

Thomas scowled. "Okay. You wear the lifejacket. We'll switch in fifteen minutes."

Claire did up the lifejacket and got in the bow. With Thomas in the stern, they pushed off into the backwater and paddled out into the current. The river was faster than they remembered from the day before, but the waves weren't as big.

After ten minutes, they came around a corner and saw a huge pile of logs stuck in the middle of the river.

"Let's pull over downstream of this logjam," yelled Thomas, "and see what we can find."

There weren't many safe places to land, so they turned the canoe upstream and paddled beside a tree trunk wedged into the logjam. The end of the tree bobbed up and down in the current.

"Hang on to a branch while I jump out," yelled Thomas.

He got out and crawled over the labyrinth of logs.

After a few moments he yelled, "Hey Claire, I found something!"

"What?"

"It might be a fanny pack or something. Yes, it is! It's all muddy." He lifted it up for her to see, then opened it up. It was a throw bag, a bag holding about twenty-five meters of rope, used for rescuing canoeists. He came back to the canoe and tossed it in the bottom. "If this was here, there's bound to be other stuff."

Claire smirked. "You're like the boy who was digging through a pile of manure and when asked what he was doing said, 'There's got to be a pony here somewhere!'"

"Very funny," said Thomas. "I'll have the last laugh, you'll see."

He climbed over the logs to the far side. Claire didn't see or hear from him for several minutes and became worried. She studied the bobbing tree beside the canoe and wondered why it was bobbing faster and higher than when they had first arrived.

"Hey, Claire! Jackpot!" shouted Thomas.

"What? What is it?" called Claire.

"It's a duffle bag! Hang on. It's stuck."

"Just hurry, Thomas! This log is acting really weird."

Thomas finally appeared with a burgundy duffle bag. He had a smile a mile wide.

"Get a load of this pony!" he gloated, throwing the bag in the canoe. He climbed in the stern and opened the bag. Everything was soaked: a pair of running shoes, a hoodie, a toque, a bag of mouldy trail mix, some wind pants, a down sleeping bag, and a camera. The camera was in a waterproof bag. Thomas' eyes grew large.

Before he could say anything, Claire shouted, "Thomas! This bouncing tree seems like it's moving!"

Thomas saw that she was right. The water was rising and the jammed log began to float away. It was no longer bobbing, but rolling with the current and banging against the side of the canoe.

"Let's get going!" yelled Thomas. "Do a high brace! Come on! Let's go!"

With her paddle, Claire pulled the bow of the canoe out into the current and turned it downstream. There was a stretch of fairly calm water ahead.

"Keep us heading straight, Claire. I'm going to see if the batteries in this camera are any good."

He took the camera out of the waterproof bag and removed the batteries. They were dry. He put them in the Transporter.

Thomas reached toward Claire. "Okay Claire, touch my hand. Let's get out of here." Claire turned and stretched until she touched Thomas' hand. He pushed the Activator. Nothing happened.

Claire frowned at Thomas. "Why am I not surprised?"

"Why am I not surprised?" Thomas repeated, imitating

her. He stared at the Transporter, trying to figure out why it wasn't working.

Claire resumed paddling to keep the canoe straight. "The current's picking up," she observed. She stopped paddling for a moment. "Thomas, do you hear that?"

"What?"

Claire turned her head to one side. "That noise."

Thomas lifted his head, then dropped his jaw. "Doesn't sound good."

"What do you mean?"

He gulped. "Sounds like I gotta get this thing working."

"Why? What is it? Thomas! What is it!"

Thomas lifted his head and his eyes narrowed. "It sounds like a waterfall. Don't bug me right now. I'm busy."

Claire turned downstream, then back to Thomas. "Is that thing going to work?"

"I hope so!"

The low rumble of the approaching falls seemed to vibrate the river itself.

Thomas raised his voice. "Why don't we change positions in the boat? It's my turn to wear the lifejacket. I think fifteen minutes are up!"

"Just get that stupid Transporter working!" Claire commanded.

The roar of the falls became even louder. Claire could see a horizontal line across the river in front of her, about two hundred meters away.

"Thomas, hurry!" she begged.

Thomas took the batteries out of the Transporter and rubbed the end of each battery on his leg. He'd heard somewhere that doing so could remove corrosion, corrosion that might prevent the battery from working. He slipped them back into the Transporter.

"Okay, Claire! Oh... wait." He had put one battery in backwards.

The falls were thundering. Claire could see the spray on the downstream side.

"Hurry, Thomas! Hurry!"

Thomas took out the backwards battery, but then dropped it in the bottom of the canoe. He picked it up, his hands shaking, and dried it off on his shirt. He carefully put it in the Transporter.

"Hang on, Claire!" he yelled.

She reached back and touched Thomas' hand as he pushed the Activator with his other hand. The bow of the canoe dipped over the edge of the waterfall and fell end over end into the cascade below.

Thomas and Claire flew through the air, their clothes soaked with spraying mist. The roar of the waterfall was deafening, but then grew softer. There was a faint, high-pitched siren sound as they somersaulted, head over heels, the air rushing past them quietly. This went on for a long time.

Suddenly, the air became warm and started to stink. The smell almost made them sick.

Claire landed on sand. Thomas landed some distance away in a muddy pond. When he came to the surface, he smelled the worst stench ever.

Discussion Questions

What do Thomas and Claire find in their backpacks?

Thomas spills the can of water in the fire and then he and Claire have an argument. Who won the argument? Who ever wins an argument?

How do Thomas and Claire get their canoe out of the river?

Thomas and Claire discuss who should wear the lifejacket. Do you agree with their logic? Why or why not?

Things seemed pretty hopeless at times for Thomas and Claire. What did they do to overcome their feelings of hopelessness?

At the end of the chapter, Thomas and Claire were transported to a new location. Where do you think they are now?

chapter 10

The water in the pond was deep enough to break his fall, but shallow enough that when Thomas stood up his feet touched the bottom. The water came up to his chest. He wiped his face with his hand and called for Claire but couldn't see her anywhere.

The pond was a dirty brown colour and not much bigger than a swimming pool. It was so dirty that he couldn't see his hands just below the surface. Aware that he was sinking in the muddy bottom, he tried to pull his feet out. They were stuck. His left foot came loose. When he finally got his right foot out, his shoe stayed behind. The pond was too murky to dive for it so he just swam toward shore, keeping his face above the water.

There were six or eight water buffalo at one end of the pond. At the other end, some dark-skinned people filled clay pots and plastic jugs with the dirty water.

The strong smell took Thomas back to the day he had come upon a dead cow while walking through the bush on his uncle's farm. It had been dead for some weeks and the smell was unbearable, even at a distance. This time the smell was worse. Far worse.

Then he saw it. On the shore in front of him lay a carcass. It was a dead water buffalo. Its head lay in the water and the rest of the bloated carcass had sunk partway into the mud. Flies swarmed over the rotting body.

When Thomas reached the edge of the pond, he thought he was going to vomit. He ran along the mucky beach, nearly losing his other shoe, and up a small hill where a slight breeze came toward him. He breathed deeply. The air was fresher, but hot.

Thomas noticed a burlap sack lying nearby. He picked it up carefully with two fingers. It was torn and dirty. Inside he found a small towel, about the size of a baby blanket. It looked more like a rag, with holes and stains.

"Well, this is sure useful!" he fumed, throwing the towel on the ground.

He also found a small plastic bag of raisins in the bottom of the sack. They seemed a bit mushy, but he didn't care; he was hungry. He opened the bag but closed it right away. The raisins had gone bad.

Where's Claire? he wondered as he scanned the area.

Nearby, a hodgepodge of tents covered the ground like a small city. Some were made of canvas, but most were made of sheets of plastic. People milled around everywhere. Small fires here and there gave the air a smoky scent. The sun blazed down and Thomas wished he had a hat. He wondered if he might get sunburn through the holes in his dirty t-shirt.

He sat down on a rock.

Now what am I supposed to do?

Even though his t-shirt and shorts were wet, he began to sweat. He stared at the towel he had thrown on the ground, then picked it up and fashioned it into a kind of hat, tying each corner with a knot so it would stay on his head.

"I've got to find Claire," he told himself as he walked back to the pond.

People were moving back and forth from the tents to the pond, filling containers with muddy water. He held his right hand above his eyes and searched the area all the way to some hazy hills a kilometer away. He couldn't see Claire anywhere. He hoped she was alright.

"Claire! Cllaaaaaiiiire!"

A man and boy filling a pail with water stopped and looked at Thomas, then continued their task. Thomas got another whiff of the dead water buffalo and walked quickly toward the tent city. He wished he was home.

Thomas tried talking with people he met, but no one spoke English. They turned away when he asked if they'd seen a girl with blond hair.

I'd better keep looking, he thought, working his way through the twisting paths that meandered around the tents.

Garbage covered the rocky ground. Thomas, missing his shoe, was careful where he stepped with his right foot.

The smell of cooking, spices, toilets, animals, canvas, smoke, and who knows what else blended together. Sometimes it was too much to bear and he took the towel off his head to cover his mouth and nose. The towel didn't smell much better.

People huddled around small fires, boiling dirty pond water in blackened pots. Very skinny people lay on mats, flies walking over their eyelids. Mothers stared blankly at nothing, holding small babies with orange-tinged hair.

Thomas walked around for two hours, until the sun began to set.

I hope Claire's alright, Thomas thought. *I'm sure she'll be fine. She's probably worrying about me. I'm okay. I'm going to be okay.* It was getting dark fast. *I better find a place to sleep.*

He found a sandy spot to lie down in the middle of a rocky field near some tents. The sand was hard but warm.

The air cooled down. Thomas' right foot was cold, so he took off his left shoe and put both feet in the burlap sack. His shirt, damp from sweat, also felt cold, so he took the towel off his head, untied the four knots, and covered himself with it as best he could. He shivered and fell asleep, wondering why he had never thought before about how comfortable his bed was at home.

* * *

Just before the sun rose, Thomas woke up, hugging his knees and shivering. The towel had fallen off during the night, so he covered himself with it again. He felt stiff and sore and dirty. His stomach growled. He opened the bag of raisins, but decided against eating them and put them back in the burlap sack. He tied knots in the corners of the towel and covered his head.

About fifty meters away, some children were picking leaves off a small bush and eating them. He stuffed his shoe in the burlap sack and walked over to the children. He was taller than them and, he didn't realize, just as dirty. The bush they ate from had thorns, so Thomas had to be careful when he pulled off the diamond-shaped leaves. He tried eating one. It tasted awful, like eating a dried lemon rind mixed with sour milk. He was about to spit it out when a little girl held up another leaf for him to eat. She ate one first.

Thomas smiled weakly, took the leaf, said "Thank you," and ate it. He shuddered, picked up his burlap sack, and headed off.

"I've got to get a drink," he gasped.

He spent the next three hours walking through the tent city. Sometimes he felt like he was going in circles.

The sun rose hot and glowed like a heat lamp overhead. His tongue sometimes stuck to the inside of his cheeks.

Finally, he came across some boys carrying pots of water on their heads. They weren't coming from the pond, but from a hill in the opposite direction. Thomas saw three ladies carrying empty pots on their hips, walking toward the hill, so he followed them. They chattered excitedly.

After ten minutes, they came to a flat area where a crowd of people surrounded a hand pump. Someone was pumping water. The rusty machine made a *scre-EEch, scre-EEch, scre-EEch* sound with each pump of the handle.

That's when Thomas saw Claire. She stood beside an old lady with weathered brown skin and wisps of scraggly hair. The lady wore a tattered dress that looked like it had been made from a piece of canvas. She held a pot and stood bent over as if her back hurt.

"Claire!" he shouted, running over to her. He wrapped his arms around her and they hugged for a long time.

"I've been searching all over for you! Where have you been?" Claire asked.

"I've been looking for you, too!" exclaimed Thomas, surprised at the dress Claire wore, woven from coarse fabric.

Claire told Thomas how she had landed on a hill of sand. She'd ended up spending the night huddled by a smoky fire with her back against that of the old lady.

"At least you had the back of someone to keep you warm," moaned Thomas. "All I had was this threadbare towel."

He took off his hat and showed it to Claire. She could see right through it.

"Claire, where are we?"

"I think this is a refugee camp."

"What's that?"

"Well, it's a place people flee to when there's a war or famine or something that makes them leave their homes. I've heard of them before. I think there are lots of them in the world."

"So where in the world do you think this is?"

"Somewhere in Africa, I'm guessing."

Thomas looked around at the myriad of tents and crowds of people. "Funny, I've always wanted to go to Africa, but I never knew this is what I'd find."

Claire told Thomas how there was excitement in the camp because two people in a jeep had come by that morning and repaired the broken water pump. That meant the refugees wouldn't have to use water from the muddy pond anymore.

"Where are these two people?" asked Thomas. "Maybe they can get us out of here!"

"They've already left."

"Did you talk with them?"

"No, I didn't get a chance. I got here just as they were leaving. Besides, Thomas, if the Transporter got us here, it will have to take us away, just like every other time."

"Well, maybe this time we won't have to use the Transporter. Maybe we can just get a ride in a jeep. I'm willing to make an exception, you know."

"Thomas, if we got a ride in a jeep, we'd be just as lost as we are now. We don't even know where we are!"

"Oh yes we do!"

"Where?"

"Some barren and rocky place with very little food or water, hot in the daytime, cold at night, sick and hungry people all over the place, and a pond with a dead water buffalo in it."

"What? A dead water buffalo? Is that why you smell so bad?"

"Very funny."

Claire leaned closer to Thomas and took a sniff. "Your breath smells awful. What have you been eating? Whatever it was, it stinks. It smells like... like lemon rind and... sour milk. Yuck!"

"I ate leaves some kids were eating earlier this morning. I didn't have anything else to eat. Except this bag of raisins that have gone bad," he complained, pulling the bag out of his burlap sack. He gave it to Claire.

She examined them closely and sighed.

"Why did they have to be raisins?" she moaned. Her stomach growled.

Just then, the old lady with the water jug appeared and said something in a hoarse voice.

Claire thought for a moment. "Here, let's rinse these raisins. They might not smell so bad then."

"Can I start with a drink?" asked Thomas.

"Let me deal with these raisins first, okay?"

"Sure."

Claire gestured for the woman to put the pot down and pour a little water into the plastic bag. Claire swished the water around and made a spout with the bag and poured the water out, keeping the raisins in. She smelled them again, then had the woman add more water. Claire repeated the process three more times before eating a raisin.

"Well?" asked Thomas, both eyebrows raised.

Claire chewed slowly, then sighed. "They're still raisins, but I think they'll be okay. Better than before they were washed, that's for sure."

She poured some raisins into Thomas' cupped hands, and some into the old woman's hands. The rest she finished herself. As Claire ate her raisins, she dropped one, bent down, and searched among the pebbles on the ground until she found it and popped it in her mouth.

Thomas had already finished his. "Not bad," he said. "But I could've eaten fifty times that much! I'm amazed you ate those. I thought you hated raisins."

"They weren't so bad," admitted Claire. "Even if they were a little off. Right now I feel rather silly always making such a fuss about raisins..."

Thomas noticed that the old lady and her water jug had vanished.

"What I really need now is a drink," he said.

There were still many people around the pump, so it took a while before Thomas and Claire got close enough to see the water coming out of a pipe attached to the pump. The pipe was about five meters long, which kept the crowd of people at the end of the pipe and away from the pump itself. The flow of water from the pipe was irregular and occasionally cloudy, but it was a lot cleaner than the pond. Thomas finally got to the pipe, filled his hands with water, and took a big drink. He did that five times. The sixth time, he splashed water on his face and used his t-shirt to dry off.

Thomas thought the skinny woman pumping the handle might faint at any moment, so he walked over and took her place. For the first few minutes he pumped rapidly and the *scre-EEch, scre-EEch, scre-EEch* sound came quickly. He watched person after person fill pails, buckets, and pots with water which now gushed out clear. After twenty minutes, the pump sounded like a donkey somewhere far away. *Scree—EEch, scree——EEch, scree———EEch...*

Sweat dripped off Thomas' face and he covered his forehead with his arm, shading his eyes from the blazing sun. A man wearing a ragged shirt took the pump handle from Thomas. The water began to flow quickly again.

Claire had a drink and walked over to Thomas.

"Let's look for the Transporter," she suggested, marching off toward the camp.

He nodded, picked up his burlap sack, and followed. "Claire?"

She stopped and turned toward him. "Yes?"

"Do you want to wear my hat?" He held out the towel with the tied corners.

"No thanks. It looks like something a pirate would wear. It suits you better. You wear it."

Thomas put the towel back on his head. He stopped, scratched his armpit, and cleared his throat. "Arggh, matey! Well then, here's a jolly thing that'll work as a bonnie bonnet fer yer golden curls, m'lady. Arggh!"

He took the shoe out of his burlap sack, then held the sack in the palm of his hands. "Latest fashion from Paree, me lovely. This burlap sun bonnet is all the rage amongst the wimen folk in Paree. Sure to turn heads." Thomas bent down on one knee and handed the sack to Claire.

She put it on her head like a toque, and curtsied.

"You got that right, Long John," she agreed.

After an hour of walking around the tent city, seeing things they would rather not have, smelling smells they couldn't identify, and hearing language they didn't understand, they came across two boys playing with sticks. Both boys wore only a pair of dirty shorts. They each had a stick about half a meter long which they used to hit a small rock into the air. They tried to see how many times they could hit the rock before it fell to the ground. They were laughing and joking, their white teeth contrasting with their dark skin, having great fun until one boy's rock spun wildly through the air and hit Thomas on the head. It didn't really hurt, but when he saw the two boys freeze he said "Ouch!" with a grin on his face.

The boys burst out laughing and one of them handed Thomas a stick. Thomas picked up the rock at his feet and hit it into the air with the stick. He hit it four times before it fell to the ground. The two boys cheered and patted him on the back, talking with excitement.

One boy pointed to himself and said "Aru," then pointed to the other boy and said "Merga."

"Aru, Merga," said Thomas. "I'm Thomas and this is my sister Claire."

"*Naratoosy*," said Aru with a big grin on his face. "Tum-es Clor."

"Uh, that's Thomas. I'm Thom–mas," he repeated, pointing to himself. Then, pointing to Claire, he said, "Claaairrrre."

Merga smiled. "*Naratoosy*."

"*Naratoosy*," echoed Thomas and Claire, hoping that what they had just said meant "hello."

"Say, have either of you guys seen a Transporter?" asked Thomas.

"Thomas, they don't understand what you're saying!" scolded Claire.

Thomas frowned at her. "It looks like this," he explained, using the stick to trace the shape of the Transporter in the sand.

Both Aru and Merga looked at the drawing and shook their heads. Thomas drew a circle on the side of the Transporter to show the Activator button. Aru stood straight and exclaimed, "*Mera samba!*" before running off into the tent city. In a minute, he came back with a sheet of plastic about two meters square. It had a hole the size of a football. Aru had a big smile on his face as he handed it to Thomas.

Thomas looked at the plastic, then at Claire, then back to Aru. "Thank you. Uh... thank you very much." He scratched his head. "Let's try this again," he said, drawing another picture in the sand.

This time he drew himself holding the Transporter. He drew the two eggbeaters on the top, then looked at Aru and Merga. Aru shrugged his shoulders and Merga shook his head.

Just then, someone in a nearby tent called out. Aru and Merga shouted back and ran toward the voice, waving at Thomas and Claire as they left.

Thomas sighed. "Do you think this plastic belongs to somebody?"

"Well," replied Claire, "we have no way of finding out, do we?" She looked at the sun in the sky. "Let's keep looking for the Transporter."

They spent the rest of the day wandering around. More times than they could have imagined, they saw mothers with sickly children and older people lying on the ground, very still. Sometimes the pungent smells were unbearable. The tent city seemed to go on forever, with each new scene a repeat of the last.

Often they stopped looking for the Transporter to help someone. Once Thomas helped an old man carry a heavy pot of water. Claire helped comfort a crying child whose mother looked very tired. She put damp cloths on the foreheads of several old people suffering from high fevers.

It was Thomas who noticed the setting sun. "We'd better find a place to sleep because it gets dark real fast here."

They found a sandy area near a group of plastic shelters. They could hear someone coughing nearby with the kind of cough that doesn't stop. Thomas and Claire wanted to go somewhere else, but there weren't many options. They got as comfortable as they could on the sand, lying back to back. Thomas gave Claire the burlap sack to put her feet in.

"I've still got shoes," she said. "You use the sack."

"I'm fine."

"Well, then wrap your feet with the towel," Claire suggested as she jammed her feet into the sack. Thomas didn't move. "Where is it?"

"I gave it away." Thomas spoke softly, resting his head on his right hand.

"To who?"

"Do you remember that woman we saw with the little baby?"

Claire didn't answer, having come across maybe a hundred women with little babies that day.

"The baby didn't have any clothes on," added Thomas.

Claire was still quiet.

"It was just before the sun got low in the sky. The baby's hair had an orange tinge." Thomas paused. "It seemed more orange than some of the other ones we saw."

Claire nodded. "Yeah. Yeah, I think I know who you mean."

"You know what was kinda scary? The baby wasn't crying. It was just lying there, breathing slowly. I gave the towel to the woman and she put it on her baby."

Thomas and Claire covered themselves with the sheet of plastic Aru had given them. The big hole was down by their legs. They were silent for a long time.

"Thomas?" said Claire quietly.

"Yeah?"

"What are you thinking about?"

"I was thinking about how hungry I am and then realized how stupid it was to think about that. I've probably eaten more in the last few days than most people in this camp have in a month. Or more." He thought for a moment. "If these people had food, blankets, medicine..." He stopped talking and chewed on his bottom lip.

The evening air cooled quickly. They were grateful for each other's warm backs, but their front sides were cool. Claire hugged her knees.

"What are you thinking about?" asked Thomas.

Claire brushed the hair off her face. "I was thinking about my music box collection."

"What about it?"

"That I really don't need any more music boxes."

"Why? Were you thinking about getting some more?"

"Yeah. When I was at home, I was. There's a really nice one in the store window at Izma's. I was thinking of buying it when I'd saved up enough money."

"Why?"

"I don't know. I guess I've always collected them."

Stars were appearing in the night sky.

Thomas rubbed his nose. "I've never understood why you collected those things."

"No, I don't suppose you would. But do you think it was wrong for me to collect so many?"

"I... don't... think it was wrong. Dumb maybe, but not wrong." He watched a shooting star streak across the sky. "Why would you think it might be wrong?"

"I don't know. Just seems funny to have a large collection of music boxes that just sit on my shelf when people are, you know, starving..."

"But there's nothing wrong with collecting stuff, is there?" asked Thomas as he hugged his knees.

"No. But I guess I could have asked myself, 'How many are enough?' I'd never thought about it before."

"You probably never thought about it before because you've never seen anything like what we've seen today."

"What do you mean?"

Thomas didn't answer for a long time. "Well, stuff like this doesn't bug people when they're not close to it, I guess."

After a while, they both drifted off to sleep, waking up now and then when one of them had shifted and their backs were no longer touching.

* * *

The next morning, Thomas and Claire woke with the sounds of the tent city, feeling like they hadn't slept at all. Someone was coughing nearby, the same person who had coughed all night.

Thomas sat up and rubbed his eyes. When he opened them, standing at his feet was the woman he had given the towel to. Tears ran down her cheeks. Thomas got to his feet. Before he could say anything, she held out the threadbare towel.

"What's happening?" asked Claire, sitting up and pushing the plastic sheet aside.

Thomas looked at Claire, then back at the woman.

"I think her baby died," he said. He swallowed to get rid of the lump in his throat. It didn't help.

He gestured for the woman to keep the towel. She stared for a moment, her face without expression, then turned and walked away.

Thomas sat down beside Claire. "I want to go home," he said, wiping a tear from his eye.

Claire was quiet. "Thomas?"

He watched the trudging woman fade into the tent city. "Yeah?"

"Even if we had the Transporter, we never know where we'll end up."

"I still want to go," sighed Thomas, head down.

"*Naratoosy!* Tum-es! Clor!" called a voice. It was Aru and Merga who ran toward them. Aru waved the Transporter above his head.

Thomas looked up and his eyes became wide. "The Transporter!" he shouted. "Oh, thank you! Thank you!"

Thomas took the Transporter in his hands. Claire put her hand on his shoulder. He was about to push the Activator when he turned to Claire and said, "Here, hold this." He handed her the Transporter, then took off his left shoe and gave it and the burlap sack to Aru.

Aru smiled. Thomas then took off his t-shirt. His eyes caught Claires.

"I didn't come with much, so it won't hurt if I don't leave with much," he explained, handing the shirt to Merga. Merga laughed and put it on.

"Let's go," said Thomas.

Claire put her hand on his shoulder as he pushed the Activator. In a split second, hot air rushed past them as they began their slow somersaulting. They heard a high-pitched siren sound as the coughing and noise of the tent city faded.

They began to hear music, soft music, the kind you hear in shopping malls. They were headed straight toward a pile of open boxes. Thankfully, the boxes were empty and cushioned their landing.

Claire was first to get to her feet. She wore black dress pants, a white blouse, and a pretty pink sweater, just like she had worn when her family went out for supper last month.

Claire wondered if she was finally home when a voice frantically called from behind her.

"And where is your brother? We're opening in three minutes and those shelves out front are not yet stocked. Where is he? Ohhhh..."

A short man with black-rimmed glasses and several pens in his shirt pocket stormed out of the room.

Discussion Questions

Describe the refugee camp.

Why does Claire wonder about buying any more music boxes?

Describe Aru and Merga. Knowing what life is like for them in the refugee camp, why do they seem to be happy?

How do you think Thomas and Claire might have changed as a result of being in the refugee camp?

At the end of the chapter, Thomas and Claire were transported to a new location. Where do you think they are now?

chapter 11

"Heymmff whhzz goiiggg ohhn?"

Claire turned to see a pair of legs sticking out of a large box. They were Thomas' legs.

"Thomas, what are you doing?"

"I'm stuff in 'ere!" Thomas' voice was muffled, his head buried in wrapping paper. Claire climbed over several empty boxes, grabbed his legs, and pulled. She fell over, hanging onto his legs, and they both ended up on the floor. Thomas had little pieces of shredded packing paper all over his head.

"Nice hairdo," observed Claire.

"Not funny," replied Thomas. "I landed on my head, you know. It's a good thing that box was full of this shredded paper stuff. I could have easily gotten hurt." He pulled some shredded paper from his hair. "Where are we?"

"I think we're in the back of some kind of store."

Thomas jumped to his feet. "What... What kind of store?" he stammered. "Do you think it's a grocery store or a restaurant? Maybe it's a convenience store that sells barbeque chicken. I sure could do with a bite to eat. A barbeque chicken would be perfect right now! But... I don't smell food. Do you smell food?"

Claire stood and brushed herself off. "I can't believe you're talking like that after just being where we were."

Thomas rubbed his neck. "Yeah. You're right. I sure forget fast."

"A short man with a tie and glasses was just here looking for you. I think you're supposed to put something on some shelves out in the front."

"So this isn't a restaurant?"

"No, I don't think so."

Thomas' shoulders sagged. "Okay, okay." He sighed. "So where's the front?"

"Well, he went that way." Claire pointed to a door. "And you'd better hurry."

"Why?"

"He said the store opens in three minutes, and that was about two minutes ago."

Thomas tucked in his shirt. "Do you have a brush or something I can use to get this packing paper out of my hair?"

"Just use your fingers."

Thomas combed the packing paper out as best he could as he walked to the door. He opened it a crack and saw a room with glass display cases. They were full of watches, perfume, jewellery, small tools, candles, books, and a variety of other items. On the far side of the room were windows and glass doors. Two dozen people stood outside, waiting to come in. Beside the door was an empty portable bookshelf, and in front of the bookshelf sat two boxes.

Those must be the shelves, he said to himself as he pushed the door open.

Thomas walked over to the bookshelf and opened the first box. It was full of books with a picture of pink, fuzzy slippers on the front. He quickly leafed through one, then started placing them on the shelves.

"No, not that way!" corrected a voice.

Thomas turned to see the short man with glasses. His collar was a bit too big and his tie was in a tight knot. He also noticed the name on his nametag: Arnie.

"Uh, Arnie, I was just—"

"It's Mr. Cheeston. And you were just what?"

"Putting these books—"

"On the shelf the wrong way!" Mr. Cheeston fumed. "The bindings must be facing out!" He straightened the books Thomas had just placed. "Now, do the other box correctly while I open the doors before these customers break them down!"

Thomas looked at the digital clock on the wall. It said nine o'clock. He tore open the next box and put a different set of books on the shelves. The cover had a picture of a cactus on the front and said "Cactus Gardens" in big letters.

Mr. Cheeston opened the doors and customers poured into the store.

"Take those empty boxes to the storage room and come man the counter," he ordered. "And get Claire out here, too."

Thomas took the boxes to the pile at the back of the store and found Claire. She was reading a thick catalogue.

"Claire, we're supposed to go help customers," he said, pointing to the front of the store. "Claire!"

"The stuff in this catalogue is *so* dumb!" she said slowly.

"Like what?"

"Like this," said Claire, pointing to a toy gun for shooting marshmallows.

"That's not dumb, that's cool!" exclaimed Thomas, snatching the catalogue out of her hands and flipping through the pages. "Look at this! It's a voice-activated robot! What an innovative idea!"

"Innovative maybe, but are those things really necessary?"

"Well, what's necessary for one person may not be for someone else." Thomas stopped flipping through the pages. "Now this is dumb," he said pointing to a pair of fluffy slippers that looked like sheep with little pink noses. "I just loaded a whole shelf with books that were all about slippers. That's dumb. Really dumb!"

"Or necessary, I guess," suggested Claire, raising an eyebrow.

Mr. Cheeston burst through the door.

"Thomas and Claire, I'm not paying you to stand around while customers are in the store. Now get to work!" he commanded, rearranging the pens in his shirt pocket.

Thomas and Claire ran out to the counters. Claire went up to an older lady wearing elegant jewellery. She wore an expensive-looking jacket and her skirt almost covered her high heels.

"Perhaps you would be so kind as to help me select a gift for my husband for our anniversary," she said in a British accent.

"Certainly. What do you think he might enjoy receiving?" Claire asked.

"That's a good question," she said thoughtfully. "What do you suggest?"

"What... does he like to do?"

The lady sighed. "He spends hours gazing out the window at the garden."

Thomas had been listening to the conversation and quickly opened the catalogue.

"What about one of these?" He showed the lady a picture in the catalogue.

"What on earth is that?" she asked.

"It's a tiny vacuum cleaner with a long tube. It's battery-operated."

She looked at him with a quizzical expression. "And whatever is it for?"

"You use it to vacuum up spiders and bugs and stuff like that."

"Oh, that! No, Walter already has one. He's only used it a few times. I wish he would use it more often. I saw a fly on the ceiling last week and he refused to get off the couch and deal with it. Quite disturbing."

"Thomas!" Mr. Cheeston called. "Please get me another box of those books about slippers. They're selling like hotcakes!"

Thomas turned to Claire, but didn't say anything. He hurried to the back of the store.

Claire scratched her head. "Well, how about this?" she suggested, pointing to a picture in the catalogue of a wall map. "It's a map of the world in the time of Columbus."

"No, I got that for him last year."

"Did he like it?"

"I guess so. He did thank me." The lady looked off into the distance for a moment. "Come to think of it, I haven't seen it since."

Claire straightened her sweater. "Does he like to read?"

"Sometimes."

"Does he have any hobbies?"

"No. Wait... he did collect butterflies when he was younger. He has a small butterfly collection in his study."

"I see," said Claire, quickly flipping to the index in the catalogue. "B, B, B... balloons, baskets, butterflies! Good!" Then turning to the lady she added, "I'll be right back."

In the storage room, Claire found Mr. Cheeston carrying a small birdbath with three yellow plastic canaries glued to the rim.

"Where would I find the book about butterflies?" she asked.

"Right over there on those metal shelves. The label on the box will tell you what's inside."

Claire found the book and hurried back to the counter. "Here's a lovely book about butterflies and how to create a garden to attract them. Do you think your husband might enjoy this?" She flipped open the pages for the lady to see and stopped at a foldout page of Monarch butterflies covering an enormous tree like frost. It was spectacular.

"Oh yes! Yes, this would be perfect! Thank you very much."

After the lady paid for the book, a man with short brown hair and a neatly trimmed beard approached the counter. He wore a designer suit, his striped tie was loose, and the top button of his collar was undone.

"How can I help you?" Claire inquired.

"I'm looking for something for my daughter for her birthday," mumbled the man in a tired voice.

"Would you like to look through our catalogue?"

"Sure."

He paged through the catalogue quickly, came to the end, then started again at the beginning.

"How old is she and what is she interested in?" Claire asked.

"She's eight. She likes to watch TV."

"What have you got for her in the past?"

"Dolls. Toys. Video games. Stuff like that."

"Did she enjoy them?"

The man thought for a moment. "Probably." He had no expression on his face.

He flipped a few more pages in the catalogue, then said, "This might do," pointing to an elegant doghouse with gingerbread woodwork on the eaves and cedar shingles on the roof. "It says here I have to order this. How long would it take to get in?"

"So, she has a dog?" asked Claire, seeing the picture of the doghouse.

"Yes. It's a cocker spaniel. No, it's a…" He stared at the ceiling for a moment. "It's a terrier, I think. Yes, a terrier. A Cairn terrier." He rubbed his chin. "Well, a terrier of some sort."

"Here's something she might like, and you can take it with you today," suggested Claire, pointing to the catalogue.

"What's that?"

"It's a leash."

"A what?"

"A leash. You know, for taking a dog for a walk."

"A leash," the man repeated.

"Yes. You could give your daughter the leash and then you both could take the dog for a walk together."

The man blinked a few times.

She continued, "I guarantee that if you go for a walk with your daughter and her dog once or twice a week, you'll have no trouble knowing what to get for her birthday next year."

A small grin appeared on the man's face. He nodded slowly. "I'll take it."

After the man bought the leash, Mr. Cheeston waved for Claire to come over and talk with him. Thomas was already there.

"This product here," said Mr. Cheeston, smiling excitedly and pointing to the catalogue, "is the CD Storage Stacker. You get a twenty percent commission for every one you sell. People aren't buying CDs anymore, so we have a pile of these stackers in the back. Make it your first suggestion to customers. We need to move them out. Here, take a closer look."

He handed the catalogue to Claire, then walked over to a tall, stylishly-dressed lady standing by the jewellery display case.

Claire read the description of the CD Storage Stacker to Thomas.

Having trouble finding that special CD? Your troubles are over with this handy and stylish 300 CD Storage Stacker. Organize your CDs with this genuine synthetic oak-veneered storage unit and spend less time looking for your favourite CDs and more time listening to them.

Claire stopped talking. She looked like she had just smelled a rotting fish. "Now this is dumb," she fumed. "No, this is outright stupid! I feel totally sick. Who needs that many CDs? After being in that refugee camp, I feel embarrassed. Try explaining this to Aru and Merga!"

Thomas stuck his pinkie finger in his ear and wiggled it around. "You know what's funny? Last summer at a garage sale I bought an eight-track stereo for one dollar. One dollar! Those things used to cost a small fortune. And I got one for a dollar!"

"What's an eight-track stereo?" asked Claire.

"It was something for listening to your favourite tunes back in the 1970s."

"Like what? Like a CD player?"

"Sort of. Only a lot bigger. I got a box of eight-track tapes with the stereo. Each one is as big as a sandwich. Nobody has them anymore. CDs are going the same way. They'll be old technology before you know it. You'll be able to buy a CD player and a box of CDs for a buck!"

Mr. Cheeston called from across the store, "Thomas, come and give me a hand."

Thomas gave Mr. Cheeston a nod, then spoke to Claire. "Don't worry. Nobody's gonna buy these CD storage things. Who has three hundred CDs anyway?"

Just then, a young man came up to the counter. He was wearing blue jeans and a tweed sports jacket with a white t-shirt underneath. He had pushed his sunglasses up on top of his head. Claire noticed he had a ring in both ears.

"How's it goin'?" he asked. "Hey, I just saw the sign in the window for the CD Storage Stacker unit." He rubbed his hands together. "I'll take two!"

Claire swallowed. "What will you do with two CD Storage Stackers?"

"Store my CDs, of course." He laughed. "What else?"

"How many CDs do you have?"

"I don't know. Must be close to... six or seven hundred. That's why I want two of those babies."

"Wow!" exclaimed Claire. "Do you... listen to them all?"

"No, not really," answered the man. "But I do need to store them better—some of them are all over the floor right now. I wish these units were higher, though, because it's going to be a little cramped putting two side by side in my living room. I could put one in the spare bedroom, though. Hmmm. Maybe I should take three. No, two will be fine for now. I can only carry two at a time anyway."

Claire went to the storage room and met Thomas carrying a plastic lawn ornament that looked like a gnome wearing sunglasses.

"Some guy with six hundred CDs is buying two of these CD Storage Stacker things," she said, taking them off a shelf.

"No way!"

"I was just thinking that if he listened to two CDs

183

every day, it would take him almost a year to listen to them all."

"That's wild!" said Thomas.

Claire shook her head. "I don't understand why he doesn't get rid of some of his CDs instead of buying more storage. He could give some away to people who might actually listen to them."

"Maybe he likes collecting CDs, just like you like collecting music boxes."

"I don't think I want to do that anymore," Claire said thoughtfully.

Thomas bent down and did up his shoelace. "How much are those stacker things anyway?"

"$129.95," answered Claire. She sighed. "Can you help me carry these two out to the front?"

"Sure, but just wait a moment while I take this 'Cool Dude Gnome' to Mr. Cheeston." Thomas took the lawn ornament out to the counters, wondering how long it would be before he saw a CD Storage Stacker at a garage sale.

Later on, Mr. Cheeston found Thomas and Claire in the back of the store. "Good job on the CD Storage Stackers! I saw you sell two to that man in the tweed jacket. Good job!" He clapped his hands together, then walked out to the front of the store beaming.

Thomas rubbed his chin. "I think I understand what you mean, Claire. It seems that people buy a lot of stuff they probably don't need."

He picked up a catalogue and thumbed through it. He stopped on a page of action figures and his eyes grew wide.

"Hey! Look at this!" he gushed. "I didn't know we sold Roger Rangerman and Carlo the Cattle Rustler. These guys are amazing! I don't have them yet. Look at Carlo's rope! And real moving spurs! And Roger has a real badge that says 'Sheriff'! This is absolutely awesome!"

"Thomas," sighed Claire, rolling her eyes, "what did you just tell me? How many more action figures do you need? You already have so many you don't know where they are half the time."

"But I don't have these guys yet. Maybe I can get an employee discount or something. Will you look at those spurs!"

Claire put her hands on her hips. "What would you say if I told you I wanted to buy another music box?"

"Well, now *that* would be ridiculous!" exclaimed Thomas. "Especially after what we just went through in that refugee camp."

"Thomas James!" rebuked Claire. "These action figures are no different than music boxes, and you know it."

"Oh, come on, Claire! These action figures are nothing like music boxes. There's no comparison. Seriously, who would ever want a music box anyway?"

Claire turned away, crossed her arms, and sighed.

Thomas flipped the page, expecting to see more action figures. His mouth dropped open, and stayed open, but he didn't speak. Finally, in a low whisper, he said, "Claire!"

Claire didn't move. "What?" she snapped, her arms still crossed.

Thomas closed his mouth and swallowed.

"What?" asked Claire again, turning. She saw the look on his face. "What? What's the matter?"

Thomas held the catalogue for her to see. She gasped. "The Transporter! In the catalogue? How... how much is it?"

"Five hundred dollars!" stammered Thomas. "If I'd known they were that valuable, I would have built a pile of them and made a fortune!"

"Where are we going to get five hundred dollars?"

Thomas furiously read the catalogue. "It doesn't say anything about ordering it, so it must be in the store somewhere. We don't need five hundred dollars. We just need to find it, then get out of here."

Mr. Cheeston poked his head through the door. "Customers out front," he announced before vanishing back into the store.

"Go and look for the Transporter," Claire whispered to Thomas as she walked out to the counter. "And hurry!"

Thomas searched every shelf in the back of the store and was about to give up when he saw it sitting on the Shipping/Receiving desk. He picked it up and decided to check the batteries. There were none.

Claire returned. "Oh good, you found it! Great! We've got to get out of here fast. There's a man at the counter who wants to buy a tea kettle that whistles 'Edelweiss' when it boils. Push the Activator. Let's go!"

"But there's no batteries!" Thomas wailed.

"Maybe there's some in the store somewhere."

"I haven't seen any the whole time we've been here. We've got to…"

Mr. Cheeston walked by quickly with a box under each arm. "Customers out front. Let's get moving!"

"Uh, Mr. Cheeston, do we sell batteries here?" asked Thomas.

Mr. Cheeston stopped. "No, but I'm thinking that would be a good idea. I just had a request for that innovative battery-powered coffee stir stick. And two requests for that battery-powered disco ball. Now, both of you get out to the counters! There are customers waiting out front and more looking in the windows. They might be coming in the store any moment," he chortled, a big smile on his face. "And don't forget to push those CD Storage Stackers!"

"What's a disco ball?" Thomas asked Claire once Mr. Cheeston had left.

"Thomas, we've got to get out of here! Now!" exclaimed Claire.

"This place isn't that bad. At least there aren't bombs exploding all around us."

"I don't care! I can't stand it any longer!"

"I told you, we don't have any batteries for the Trans..." Thomas stopped talking and pointed to the Shipping/Receiving bench. "Hey, look, there's a flashlight!"

He walked over and turned it on. It had a bright beam. He took out the batteries.

"Great! Double-As," he exclaimed as he installed them into the Transporter.

"Customers in the store!" called Mr. Cheeston.

"Hurry, Thomas! Hurry!" pleaded Claire as she placed her hand on his shoulder.

Thomas pushed the Activator.

There was a faint, high-pitched siren sound. Both Thomas and Claire began to slowly spin through the air. They thought they heard Mr. Cheeston say something about two customers wanting CD Storage Stackers...

Snowflakes filled the rushing air. After a while, Thomas and Claire felt like they were in a snow storm.

Then, with a thud, they landed facedown in a pile of snow. Claire lifted her head and wiped off the snow. She got to her knees. A strong wind blew biting ice crystals in her face.

"Thomas? Thomas! Are you okay?"

Thomas dug the snow from his collar as he stood up. "Yeah, I'm okay. Why did we have to land so hard?"

Claire rose to her feet. "*Now* where are we?"

It was daytime, but the sky was overcast and snow fell heavily. The wind whistled around them. Thomas thought he could see the faint outline of a mountain.

"I don't know," he said. "One thing I do know: this is definitely no tropical resort."

Suddenly a voice from behind called, "Hey! What are you doing out here in this storm? Why aren't you in your tent?"

Discussion Questions

Describe the three people Claire helped at the counter, and how she helped them.

What do you think of Thomas' conclusion that some of the items in the catalogue were dumb, except when it came to Roger Rangerman and Carlo the Cattle Rustler?

After a while Claire couldn't stand being in the store, having just come from the refugee camp. Why do our experiences sometimes affect how we feel about things?

Can you think of a time when you or someone you know had a changed outlook on life after an experience they had?

At the end of the chapter, Thomas and Claire were transported to a new location. Where do you think they are now?

chapter 12

Thomas and Claire turned to see who had spoken. A tall man in a red hooded snow jacket and wind pants stood nearby. A black balaclava covered his face.

They brushed the snow off themselves and noticed they wore expensive-looking hooded jackets and pants, mitts, and snow boots. Mountaineering packs lay on the ground beside them, as well as the Transporter. Thomas picked it up, knocked the snow from it, and zipped it in an outside pocket of his pack.

Claire turned toward the man. "Uh, we're a little... disoriented in this storm. Could you direct us to... to our tent?"

"Over there." The man gestured to a small group of men. "See those Sherpas?"

Thomas and Claire peered through the falling snow. About a hundred meters away, they saw some people near a cluster of colourful tents.

"Your tent is the orange one on the right."

"Okay, thanks," said Claire.

"Yeah, thanks," echoed Thomas.

They picked up their packs. Thomas needed Claire's help to lift his onto his back. As they tramped through the fresh snow, he asked her, "What's a Sherpa?"

"I think it's someone who carries heavy loads for climbing expeditions. If there are Sherpas here, we're probably in Nepal. That's where Mount Everest is, you know."

"I thought Mount Everest was in China," wondered Thomas.

"Well, that's true. It's on the border of Nepal and what used to be Tibet, now China."

Thomas nodded his head. "How do you know all this stuff?"

"I dunno. I just sorta pick it up as I go along."

"Well, I've been going along and I ain't picked up stuff like that."

"Maybe you should read more and goof around less."

"What do you mean, *goof around less*? Building the Transporter isn't what I would call *goofing around*. If it weren't for me, we wouldn't even be here right now!"

"Exactly."

As Thomas and Claire trudged through the snow, they came over a small rise and saw their tent surrounded by many others, scattered among boulders and piles of snow. It looked like a crowded campground on the May long weekend. They unzipped the door of their tent and crawled inside. Thomas opened up his pack.

"Look at this!" he exclaimed, showing Claire a coil of climbing rope. "And this!" He held up a lightweight mattress pad. "You can lie on one of these mattresses on ice and snow and not even know it!" He dropped the mattress pad, then held up a sleeping bag. "I've always wanted one of these! They're the latest expedition sleeping bags! Good to minus thirty-five degrees!"

Before Thomas could show her anything else they heard footsteps outside the tent. A man with an Australian accent called, "Supper in ten minutes. Come prepared for a planning meeting."

"Sure. What... are we planning tonight?" Claire asked through the tent wall.

"Load plan to Camp 2."

"Right," nodded Claire. She didn't have a clue what he was talking about. "And where is the meeting?"

"In the mess tent."

"Gotcha." Claire shook her head in wonder. She mouthed the words *mess tent* without making a sound. When the crunching sound of the man's footsteps faded away, she whispered anxiously, "Let's get out of here before we get mixed up in something. Thomas, take out the Transporter!"

Thomas slowly returned the climbing rope, mattress pad, and sleeping bag to his pack. "Let's stay, just a little longer."

"No. Let's go! Thomas, I *really* want to go home. I've been thinking. We've got to go home sometime and that's more likely to happen the more times we push the Activator. This might be the time!"

Thomas scowled. "I'm hungry! Let's have supper at least. We'll leave... right after dessert!"

"That's ridiculous," argued Claire. "If all you're concerned about is food, you can eat when we get home. Mom and Dad must be terribly worried about us. Let's leave right now!"

"We don't know that," argued Thomas.

"We don't know what?"

"We don't know what time it is at home. It might still be lunchtime, but it might also be the middle of the night. Who knows? We *do* know what time it is here. It's supper-time! Now! Right at this moment! Suppertime!" Thomas licked his lips. "I vote we stay here and have supper."

Claire moved closer to Thomas. "You must be nuts!" she snapped, glaring at him. "Whatever time it is back home, it's still home and I want to be there!"

"Claire, I don't know why you're so uptight. If we were to leave right now, the Transporter could take us anywhere. We don't know if we'll go home." Thomas saw the concern on Claire's face. "I mean... *when* we'll go home."

They were silent for a moment, then Claire sniffed. This was something that had been bothering her for some time, but she didn't know what to do about it. "Thomas. What if we never go home? What if..."

Thomas saw Claire wipe a tear from her eye. He sighed. "Alright. Okay. We'll go." He unzipped the pocket on his pack and took out the Transporter. "Wait a minute. One of the FRMs is missing!" Claire's face was blank. "The other eggbeater—it's gone!"

Claire looked closely at the Transporter. "Didn't you notice it was missing when you put it in your pack after we landed?"

"No."

"Did it break off inside that pocket?"

Thomas dug around in his pack. "Negative," he said.

"Maybe it broke off when we landed in the snow. Try it anyway."

Thomas pushed the Activator after Claire put her hand on his shoulder. Nothing happened.

"Thomas, it worked with only one eggbeater when we were in India. You thought we had to go to a higher elevation to make it work. I think we're at an even higher elevation now than we were then. Why isn't it working?"

Thomas checked the batteries. They seemed fine. "I don't know." He scratched his head. "Hey! How about this? Let's have supper, then go look for the other Frequency Reception Modulator right after." Claire nodded. "First, open your pack. I want to see what you got."

Besides the equipment Thomas had in his pack, Claire's pack held a book. It was thick and full of pictures of food. Claire had a quizzical look on her face. "A cookbook?"

Thomas and Claire found the mess tent by following a well-worn trail. Inside were two long tables with benches. A lantern hung over each table. Thomas and Claire joined about twenty people who were already sitting.

As food was served—large pots of rice, steaming soup, and lentil stew—Claire and Thomas learned a number of things. The men at the table were an elite group of mountain climbers from around the world, attempting an international ascent of Mount Everest. The climbing team was assisted by Sherpas, Nepali men who were smaller and darker than the climbers and who carried heavy loads and guided the climbers up the mountain.

The route up the mountain began at Base Camp, where the tents were located, and proceeded to the bottom of an immense glacier. The face of the glacier, called the Khumbu Icefall, was the cause of heated discussion. The Icefall was full of crevasses, or huge cracks in the ice, some large enough to swallow a semitrailer.

Several climbers, in turn, rose to address the group. A bearded climber with a small Russian flag sewn on his sleeve expressed concern about the constant movement of ice in the Icefall. A Spanish climber with a strong accent suggested they speed up efforts, especially when the weather was good. A short, stocky climber from France waved his hands as he described how the afternoon sun made the whole route dangerous—the risk of avalanches was extreme.

Suddenly everyone talked at once. Thomas leaned over to the climber beside him and found out that the team had already established tentsites, called Camps, partway up the mountain. Camp 1 was about two kilometers past the dangerous Icefall, and Camp 2 was another three kilometers past that. Two more Camps would be placed further up the steep south slope of Mount Everest.

The team leader now stood up, an American with a green toque. He seemed tired and his confident smile betrayed his rising concern.

"Fellas," he said as he looked around at every face. The lanterns cast long shadows on the walls of the mess tent. "We have been doing much better recently at working together to achieve our goal. However, we now have some new challenges to deal with. Several Sherpas are ill and unable to carry loads. Heavy snowfalls have slowed the movement of supplies to the Camps. Adding to that is the increased risk of avalanches." He paused, sizing up the group. They all watched him intently. "Finally, as you all know, the route through the Icefall changes daily as the ice moves, opening new crevasses. The ice has also crushed or twisted many of the ladders we use to cross crevasses."

The whole group burst into discussion. After a few minutes, the team leader gave lengthy instructions about how the next day would be organized, and who would be doing what. There would be two climbing parties taking supplies. One would leave Base Camp at 2:30 a.m. without any loads, climb up to Camp 1, then take supplies from there to Camp 2. Afterward they would return to Base Camp. The second party would leave at 4:00 a.m. and take supplies up to Camp 1 for the following day's carry. Both groups would need to return to Base Camp before noon as the heat of the day would cause the ice in the glacier to move and the snow to become heavy.

The team leader didn't say anything about what Thomas and Claire had to do, but he did ask if there were any questions.

Thomas raised his hand. "Yes, I have one. What do you want me and my sister to do?"

Claire tugged at Thomas' sleeve. When he didn't look at her, she gave him a small kick under the table. He pretended not to notice.

"Ah yes, thank you. You two will need to take four ladders to the base of the Icefall, to be used for route repair. That should take the better part of the day. We'll all have a meeting back here tomorrow afternoon at three o'clock."

There were no further questions, so the team leader concluded, "Remember, there is to be no unnecessary travel through the Icefall after noon."

Thomas wondered why that would be a problem, but didn't say anything.

The group dispersed.

"Don't worry, old chap," said a climber with a British accent as he patted Thomas on the back. "Everyone takes a turn hauling ladders. Can't get any worse than that."

Thomas asked one of the Sherpas leaving the tent, "What time is breakfast?"

"2:00 a.m. for team one. 3:30 a.m. for team two. Since you not going into Icefall, you eat breakfast 6:00 a.m."

Thomas started walking toward his tent.

Claire caught up to him. "Have you forgotten something?"

Thomas stopped and turned. "What?"

"We need to find your eggbeater," she said angrily. "And why did you have to ask that question? You agreed we would head home right after supper, not participate in a climbing expedition!"

"Well, yeah, but don't you think this is kinda fun?"

Claire stopped walking. "Fun? No! Not at all! I want to go home, not anywhere near icefalls and avalanches!" She put her hands on her hips. "Thomas, this place is dangerous! It's no place for two kids. Especially us!"

"Oh, come on," he retorted. "We won't be going anywhere near that stuff, we'll just be carrying some ladders. It'll be fun! Imagine telling Eddy Hansen back home that we were at Everest Base Camp and helped an international expedition climb Mount Everest!" A gloating look came over his face. "He wouldn't believe us in a thousand years!"

Claire crossed her arms. "You're absolutely right about that," she agreed. "Now, let's go find that egg modulation thingy before you ask any more questions!"

As the falling snow tapered off, Thomas and Claire found the place where they had landed only two hours before. They dug around in the fresh snow with their feet.

Thomas found the eggbeater and quietly slipped it into his coat pocket without telling Claire. He pretended to keep digging for a while, then said, "Maybe someone took it already."

"Who would take an eggbeater?" asked Claire. "Come on, we've got to find it."

"I know," said Thomas. "Let's ask the cook in the mess tent if he has an extra eggbeater we can borrow."

"You mean keep."

"Yeah, right. Keep. We'll ask him... tomorrow. Right after breakfast."

Claire dug around in the snow for a moment, then yawned. "Well, if breakfast is at 6:00 a.m., we won't have long to wait. Let's go back to our tent and get some sleep. But we ask for the eggbeater right after breakfast, and not a moment later. Okay?"

"Sure. You bet."

* * *

After breakfast, Claire got up from the table to ask the cook for an eggbeater. As she approached the kitchen area of the mess tent, she stopped, frowned, turned around, and sat back down next to Thomas.

198

She spoke quietly. "Thomas, why should the cook give me an eggbeater? I don't know who the cook is and he certainly doesn't know who I am. What am I supposed to say? 'Excuse me, do you have an extra eggbeater lying around? I need one to replace a lost FRM on my brother's Transporter. Pardon me? No, I'm not crazy, and no, you'll never see your eggbeater again.'"

"Listen," Thomas said. "We're here at Everest Base Camp and we've been asked to go to the Icefall. Let's do that much and worry about the Transporter later. This is adventure to the extreme!"

Claire put her elbows on the table and rested her chin in her hands. "I've had enough adventure, thanks. I really want to go home, but for your sake, alright." She straightened up. "When we're done, *you* ask the cook for an eggbeater."

"Deal."

They each took a bagged lunch from the mess tent and prepared for their trip to the base of the Icefall. In their tent, they packed extra clothing, two liters of water, and their lunch. Thomas also stuffed the rolled mattress pad into his pack.

"Why are you bringing that sleeping pad thing?" inquired Claire.

"We can sit on it while we're eating lunch," responded Thomas. "It doesn't weigh much. Anyway, let's go get our first ladder."

The equipment supply tent was a spacious shelter full of crates and boxes and racks of climbing ropes, harnesses, clothing, ladders, and other paraphernalia. The center of the tent was held up by a long ladder instead of a pole. Thomas and Claire were surprised to learn that it had taken many days to haul the supplies to Base Camp on the backs of Nepalese porters.

They were even more surprised when they were given

their first ladder to carry to the Icefall. Claire read the label on the ladder. It was six meters long and made of aluminum. Although it only weighed fourteen kilograms, it was awkward to carry. With Thomas at one end and Claire at the other, they bumbled along the trail from Base Camp, like a comedy act on TV.

It took over an hour to get to the base of the Icefall, and from that vantage point Thomas and Claire got a clearer picture of what the climbers were up against. It looked like a gigantic pile of building blocks. Finding a route through was not only difficult, but dangerous. In the heat of the afternoon sun, the blocks of ice would shift and sometimes collapse. Some would tumble onto others, causing a domino effect.

They put the ladder in a stockpile of equipment ready to go up the glacier toward Camps 1 and 2. Beside the stockpile was another stack of ladders, twisted and bent out of shape.

"What happened to these?" wondered Claire aloud.

"I bet the Icefall smushed them up," guessed Thomas. "Remember what they were talking about last night?"

They returned to Base Camp to get another ladder, wondering what kind of force it would take to bend a ladder into a pretzel shape.

It was late morning when they arrived at the Icefall with their second ladder. It was longer and heavier than the first one, but they'd figured out a system to take steps at more or less the same time, which made it easier to carry. As they unloaded the ladder onto the equipment stockpile, a group of three climbers and four Sherpas emerged from the Icefall. They looked like they'd seen a ghost.

"How's it going?" called Thomas when the climbers came within earshot.

One of the climbers, named Jim, sat on a rock and took off his pack.

"Big movements in the Icefall," he said, taking a long drink of water. "Twice, right in front of us, a huge ten-meter block of ice tumbled across the trail. Once a block fell and smashed a ladder. We had no way to get across the gaping crevasse in front of us once the ladder was gone. It took us over an hour to work our way around 'til we finally got back on the trail. The ice kept creaking and groaning." He took a deep breath. "I'm sure glad we're here now, no question."

"Were you going to Camp 1 or Camp 2?" asked Thomas.

"Camp 2," Jim answered, wiping his face with his sleeve. "We made good time up the Icefall this morning without a load, but the trail after Camp 1 was ponderous because of the heavy snowfall last night. And now the Icefall is a nightmare! Am I ever glad we made it back when we did." He paused. "How long has the other team been back?"

"What do you mean?"

"You know, the second team bringing supplies to Camp 1. They left after us this morning and should have gotten back to camp some time ago. When did they get back?"

"We haven't seen them." Thomas scanned the glacier. "Do you think they're still in the Icefall somewhere?"

Jim opened his mouth to speak when a shout came from behind him. Everyone turned to see two Sherpas running toward them from the Icefall. They were about three hundred meters away and slipping constantly as they ran over the snow and rough blocks of ice. In a few moments, they arrived at the astonished group.

"Accident!" one of them gasped. "We stop for rest. Big ice fall down!" The Sherpa slapped his hands together. "Ice smash ladder and disappear in crevasse. Donovan trap in ice. Need help! Get rescue! Get doctor!"

"Donovan!" exclaimed Jim. He turned to Thomas and Claire. "He's the other team's lead climber." He turned to the Sherpa. "How badly is he hurt?"

"Don't know. Donovan trap under ice."

"Why didn't anyone radio us?" asked Jim.

"Both radios no work... or gone," stammered the Sherpa.

Jim turned to his climbing team and sent three of them to Base Camp for rescue equipment, more two-way radios, and extra help. He was just describing what he and his remaining team members would do when the rumble of an avalanche on the south face of Everest interrupted him. The roar of rushing snow increased in volume and finally subsided. Flying snow drifted through the air along the slopes for some time.

"Let's go before things get worse!" he commanded.

Thomas and Claire were left standing, watching the climbers disappear in two directions, three to Base Camp, and Jim and six others back into the Icefall.

"Now what?" asked Claire. She didn't wait for an answer. "Thomas, let's leave. It's neat here and everything, but this is too much for me. I don't like how this is turning out. Let's go, Thomas. Please?"

"I left the Transporter in our tent," remembered Thomas.

"Well, let's go get it!"

Thomas rubbed his chin. "Tell you what," he begged, grabbing Claire's arm. "You get it and bring it back here. I'll hang around to see if I can help. When you show up, we'll try the Transporter."

Claire nodded slowly. "Okay."

She picked up her pack and hiked back down the trail toward Base Camp. It didn't take her long to catch up to the climbers.

Thomas sat on a flat rock where he could see the trail

leading to Base Camp. After an hour or so, a group of about twelve climbers and Sherpas from Base Camp appeared in the distance, walking quickly and carrying rescue and climbing gear. They reached Thomas just as two more climbers appeared from the Icefall, out of breath.

When they were all together, one of the out-of-breath climbers updated everyone and described the best route to the accident. His sentences were short as he caught his breath. He ended by saying that there was a small opening in the ice, like a tunnel, leading to Donovan. The opening of the tunnel was too small for any climber to fit through, or even one of the smaller Sherpas. Concern covered his face as he spoke. Then his eyes fell on Thomas.

"You!" he exclaimed, pointing at Thomas. "You could maybe fit in the opening! Quick, put on a harness!"

Thomas was handed a climbing harness, which he stepped into and snugged up around his waist. Then someone handed him some crampons. They looked like sandals with metal spikes on the bottom. He stared at them, not sure what he was supposed to do. A Sherpa walked over and helped strap them to his boots. Next, they gave him an ice axe with a pointy end and t-shaped handle.

In a few moments, he was ready to go. He grabbed his pack and set off with the rest of the rescue team.

The trail through the Icefall was terrible. Mammoth blocks of ice, some fifteen meters tall, towered precariously over the climbers. Ladders, some with rope handrails, crossed gaping crevasses. Some ladders were twisted and bent at strange angles. While crossing one of these ladders, Thomas looked down. The blue ice darkened to black the further he looked. He couldn't see the bottom.

Sections of the trail involved clipping his harness to a fixed climbing rope, jamming his crampons into the steep snow slope and slowly working his way along. Whenever the trail hugged an ice block, he chopped into it with his ice axe to keep from falling. Sweat ran down his neck. By now, the sun was directly overhead. Every so often an ominous creaking would signal the nearby movement of an ice block. Sometimes a block shifted only a little; sometimes it toppled and crashed into a thousand pieces.

After an hour and a half, the trail led the rescue team along the bottom of an enormous open slope covered in deep snow. The group split up and crossed in twos. They kept looking up the slope, but Thomas couldn't figure out why.

Shortly after crossing the slope, they arrived at the accident scene. The ground was littered with equipment. People were lying here and there, some injured, some dazed. The rescue team placed a Sherpa with a broken leg on a stretcher. His leg had been splinted with an ice axe and taped in place. Two Sherpas and two climbers picked up the stretcher and began the dangerous and difficult descent back across the open snow slope and through the Icefall to Base Camp.

Thomas was led to the ice tunnel. A Sherpa gave him a headlamp and one of the climbers tied a rope to his harness. Thomas peered into the tunnel. It was barely big enough to crawl through. He couldn't see more than a meter past the entrance.

"Are you sure someone's in there?" he asked hesitantly.

"Absolutely. Name's Donovan Hodgson. He's our Canadian climber. We thought he called us about an hour ago, but we haven't heard anything since."

Thomas looked at the faces staring hopefully at him. "What do you want me to do if I find him?" he asked.

"Give him some of this," said a climber, handing Thomas a thermos. "And reassure him. We need to know exactly where he is so we can reach him by the shortest route possible. That's where you come in."

Thomas nodded, unstrapped his crampons, and got down on his hands and knees.

"Pull on the rope when you want help," said someone. "Pull twice if you're coming back out and want us to take up the slack. Pull three times if you need help to get out. We'll give you a hand."

"Right," said Thomas, wondering what he was getting himself into. He crawled on his belly, pushing the thermos and ice axe in front of him. The white snow and clear ice magnified his headlamp beam and lit up the tunnel like a floodlight. His back regularly scraped along the low ceiling.

At one point, only three meters from the entrance, a block of ice jutted into the side of the tunnel and Thomas didn't think he could squeeze through. He had to shimmy along on his side, which meant he only had one arm to pull his body along.

After five or six meters, the tunnel dropped slightly and made a sharp left turn. There, lying on his side, was a man. He was only inches from the edge of a crevasse big enough to swallow him whole.

"Mr. Hodgson? Mr. Hodgson?" Thomas called. He waited for a response and wondered if the man was dead, then noticed his chest moving slowly up and down.

"Can you hear me?"

Donovan lifted his head slightly. His eyes didn't focus. He mumbled something, then dropped his head back onto the ice.

Thomas sized up the situation. There was little room to move around and his head touched the ice ceiling when he was on his hands and knees. A block of ice the size of a television lay on Donovan's legs. It was too heavy to move, so Thomas hacked at it with his ice axe and threw the chunks down the crevasse. They hit something after three or four seconds.

While lifting a large awkward block, something fell out of Thomas' coat pocket, rolled along the ice into the crevasse and disappeared, making a pinging sound as it hit the steep ice walls below. It was the eggbeater. His face went blank, realizing what had just happened.

That's the least of my problems right now, he thought.

Donovan wasn't bleeding, and Thomas was thankful for that. The sun had been hot just before the accident and Donovan had stripped down to a t-shirt and light vest. Thomas realized Donovan must be freezing to death, having lain on the ice all this time. He had to get Donovan warm. The hot drink in the thermos would help, if he could get it into him.

He poured a cup and gently held Donovan's head. Donovan took a few sips, then lay back down. Thomas put his toque on the ice and rested Donovan's head on it.

Then Thomas remembered the mattress pad in his pack. If he could get Donovan on it somehow, that might keep him alive long enough to be rescued. Thomas left the thermos and ice axe and gave the rope two tugs. As he crawled along the tunnel, someone at the entrance pulled up the slack.

When Thomas reached the narrow part of the tunnel, it somehow seemed tighter than before and took a lot more effort to pull himself through. A sea of expectant faces greeted him when he reached the opening.

"He's alive," explained Thomas as he emerged, brushing snow off his pants and coat, "but seems injured. He's about ten meters that way, sloping down." He pointed in the approximate direction. "Right alongside that crevasse over there, but surrounded by a pile of ice blocks. Right now I need my pack. I have a mattress pad that I might be able to get under him until he's rescued." Someone handed Thomas his pack. He took out the mattress pad and crawled back into the tunnel.

This time it was nearly impossible to squeeze through the narrow part and Thomas almost got stuck.

What's going on? he wondered. *Why is this so tight?*

He could feel sweat on his forehead as he struggled to get through, even though the air felt like a refrigerator. Finally Thomas reached Donovan, who hadn't moved.

"Donovan, I've got a mattress pad here for you to lie on. Do you think you could move over onto it?" Thomas rolled out the mattress pad. Thinking Donovan might fall into the open crevasse, Thomas pulled on Donovan's vest and inched him onto the pad. "Tell me if this hurts too much. I'll try and help you."

It took a few minutes, but eventually Donovan lay on his side on the mattress pad. Thomas supported his neck the whole time.

Donovan's winced and said, "Arm."

Thomas examined Donovan's right arm. It didn't seem normal, bent at a funny angle. He thought it might be broken, but continued to focus his efforts to warm Donovan. He filled the cup from the thermos and supported Donovan's head. He drank slowly, slurping as if his lips were frozen.

Soon the cup was empty. The combination of the mattress pad and the hot drink caused Donovan to wake out of his stupor enough to sit up a little on the sloping tunnel floor. He opened and closed his eyes several times, then began to talk.

"Who… who are you?"

"My name's Thomas. I'm here to help you. Where does it hurt?"

Donovan blinked a few times. "Arm," he groaned,

feeling his right arm. Then he felt his right shoulder. "Shoulder. Head hurts."

"There's a whole bunch of people working to get you out of here."

Thomas poured Donovan another drink; he drank half the cup, then spoke slowly. "Thomas, would you..." He swallowed. "Would you do something... for me?"

"You bet," said Thomas. "What do you need?"

"I... might not get out of here and—"

"Oh no, you'll be okay," interrupted Thomas. "Don't... talk like that."

Donovan smiled a little, then turned serious. "I need you to..." He took a laboured breath and grimaced in pain. "...give a message to my wife." He inhaled through his nose. "Tell her that I love her."

"Sure. But you can tell her yourself after you get out of here." He looked into Donovan's face, the headlamp beam reflecting off the ceiling. "Anything else?"

"Yeah." Donovan put down the cup and clutched his shoulder. "Yeah, there is. Tell John..." His eyes squinted in pain. He took a deep breath and exhaled slowly.

"John?" asked Thomas.

"Our leader. Tell him I'm sorry I haven't supported him... like I should have." Donovan paused and tilted his head so he could look Thomas in the eyes. "I've been insubordinate." Seeing Thomas' puzzled face, he explained, "I've been... stubborn." Donovan's mouth opened and eyes closed tight. He took another breath. "He's actually been a great leader. I should have been a better team player. Tell him I'm sorry."

Thomas nodded. "Oh... okay. I will."

Suddenly they were interrupted by scraping and chopping sounds and muffled voices. A moment later, a headlamp beam shone from inside the crevasse. Then a head appeared. It was a member of the rescue team.

"Good directions, kid. We couldn't have got here if it weren't for you. How's Donovan?"

"Cold," Donovan mumbled.

"Good stuff. We'll get you out of here in no time. I think we can bust through that wall," explained the rescuer, pointing to a corner of the tunnel where some light filtered through the ice and snow. He picked up a two-way radio and gave some instructions, then turned to Thomas. "Well done, kid. Now, high tail it outta here."

Thomas was more than happy to comply. As he picked up his ice axe, Donovan spoke. "Thanks, Thomas."

"You're welcome." Thomas gave two tugs on the rope, then squirmed his way back down the tunnel.

The narrow part of the tunnel seemed even smaller than it had before. Thomas tried to pull himself along with his right arm, but his left shoulder jammed into the low ceiling. He tried moving backward, but this time he was stuck. Really stuck.

He tried to push with his feet, but they were wedged tight. He tried to hook the ice axe on the tunnel floor but it just slipped. He reached for the rope but couldn't pull it. Finally he twisted his chest to change his grip on the rope. It helped a little and he gave two solid tugs. He took a breath and, with all his might, pulled on the rope one more time.

The rope tightened. He still didn't move. His left leg felt like it was in a vice. Just when he thought the rope might break, he budged a little. Then a little more. Suddenly, he shot forward, leaving his left boot trapped in the ice behind him. A moment later, he was standing in the sunlight outside the tunnel with a boot on one foot and a boot liner on the other.

It took a minute before his breathing slowed down. Someone unhooked his rope.

"Thanks... for getting me out," he stammered.

A group of climbers and Sherpas were shovelling snow and chopping the ice nearby. John, the team leader, was listening to a two-way radio and giving directions.

"Excuse me, John," called Thomas. "I have a message from Donovan."

No sooner had Thomas relayed Donovan's message than he heard Claire on the slope below him.

"Thomas!" She ran up to him and threw her arms around him. "Thomas, I'm so glad you're alright. I was worried about you! I came with the backup rescue party when we heard on the radio you had gone in a tunnel to help the trapped climber." She took a breath. "Is... is he okay?"

"Yes, I think he'll be alright. Let's go."

"Do you mean go back to Base Camp, or... leave?"

Thomas looked sheepish. "We can't leave," he said.

"Why not?"

"I had the missing Frequency Reception Modulator the whole time. I found it when we went back and dug around in the snow. I didn't want to let you know because I didn't want to leave right away. But I lost it. Down that crevasse over there," he said, pointing behind him. He looked down at the ground. "I shouldn't have been so selfish, Claire. I'm... sorry."

Claire grinned. "Oh. Thomas!" she giggled. "You know what I did? I went to the camp cook and got two eggbeaters, so now we can definitely leave!" She reached into her pack and pulled out two shiny eggbeaters and the Transporter.

Thomas' chuckled. "These are perfect. How did you get them? I mean, how did you ask for them?"

"I remembered I had a cookbook in my pack, so I made a trade with the cook," she explained, looking pleased. "It was just what he wanted. He was thrilled! He tried to give me a frying pan, too!"

Thomas gave Claire a hug. She handed him the Transporter and eggbeaters.

"Let's move down the trail away from everyone before we try it," he said.

"But Thomas, you only have one boot on! What happened?"

"I'll tell you later. Let's go. This boot liner should last me a few more minutes."

They left the rescue area and went another hundred meters along the twisting trail, past a graveyard of ice blocks to the open snow slope.

"I don't think we should stop here, Thomas," said Claire, shaking her head. "One of the Sherpas told me it was dangerous. This is an avalanche slope."

"It's dangerous everywhere around here. Besides, we'll be out of here before you know it."

He began hooking up one of the new eggbeaters into the Transporter. The eggbeater shaft was slightly larger than the hole in the Transporter and he had trouble getting it to fit. Just as he finished, a loud *woof* sound shattered the air. Thomas looked high up the slope to see a wall of snow cascading toward them.

"A–Avalanche!" yelled Claire. "Thomas, it's an avalanche! Push the Activator! Push the Activator!"

"It's jammed! It's not working!" Thomas frantically pounded the Activator with his fist. He could feel the wind in front of the avalanche careening toward them.

"Thomas! Thomas!" yelled Claire, her voice fading in the rushing wind.

The air was full of blowing snow. Before they knew it, they began a slow, head-over-heels somersaulting motion. They both felt dizzy. They could hear a faint, high-pitched siren sound.

The air slowly cleared and rushed past them quietly. This seemed to go on for a long time before the air brightened, becoming warm and humid. They could hear seagulls in the distance.

They landed with a thud, flat on a hot sandy beach. Waves lapped gently against the shore nearby. Claire saw a group of people playing volleyball. Nearby, a tall palm tree shimmered gently in the breeze.

Thomas spat sand out of his mouth. "Remind me to close my mouth next time I push the Activator."

Behind them came a voice, in a slight British accent. "Excuse me?"

Thomas and Claire turned to see a black-haired man dressed like a waiter. He wore black pants, a white shirt, a black bowtie, and white gloves. He had one hand under a silver tray that held tall glasses with white straws and pieces of lemon stuck on the rims. His other hand was behind his back. He tilted his head slightly.

"Excuse me, but would you prefer the pineapple colada or the mango passion fruit beverage this afternoon?"

Discussion Questions

What concerns/problems did the expedition leader discuss at the meeting?

Why did the leader not want any unnecessary travel in the Icefall after noon?

What messages did Donovan want Thomas to relay? Why?

What did Thomas do that might affect Claire's trust in him?

Is it hard or easy to ask someone for forgiveness? Why or why not?

At the end of the chapter, Thomas and Claire were transported to a new location. Where do you think they are now?

chapter 13

The waiter smiled and repeated his question.

"Would you prefer the pineapple colada?" he asked, holding up a tall glass with yellow liquid, "or the mango passion fruit?" He put the first glass down and picked up one with an orange liquid.

Thomas looked at Claire, then back at the waiter. "Uh, what would you suggest?"

"Both are quite refreshing, sir, and favourable to the palette."

Thomas turned to Claire with a look on his face that said, *What did he just say?*

Claire whispered to him, "He says they taste good."

"Okay," said Thomas. "I'll have the mango fusion fruit thing, please."

"Indeed," said the waiter, handing Thomas the drink. "And you, madam?"

"I'll have the pineapple colada, please."

The waiter gave the glass to Claire, who noticed that Thomas had already finished his drink.

"Boy, is this stuff good!" Thomas exclaimed as he passed back the empty glass. "Thanks, uh... by the way, what's your name?"

"Matthew, sir. And may I inquire from you both as to your preferences for this evening's repast?"

Thomas turned to Claire for an interpretation. "He wants to know what you want for supper," she explained.

"Oh, sure," said Thomas enthusiastically. "What's on the menu?"

"Pork tenderloin with scalloped potatoes and steamed garden vegetables, or chicken cordon bleu with sautéed baby carrots and baked potato."

Thomas turned to Claire for help.

"What do you recommend, Matthew?" she inquired.

"The chicken cordon bleu is magnificent and will be a delight to your culinary senses."

"Very good then," decided Claire. "We'll have that. Thank you very much, Matthew."

"Indeed. And would you prefer your dinner brought to your villa or would you prefer to eat in the guest dining room this evening?"

"The villa would be nice," answered Thomas, not entirely sure what a villa was.

"Matthew, would you mind pointing us in the right direction?" requested Claire. "We arrived... recently and we're not entirely... familiar with..."

Matthew nodded. "Indeed." He raised his left arm and pointed along the beach. "It's the first of seven buildings, just past the volleyball court. Supper will be served shortly, at 5:30 p.m." With that, he gave a slight bow, tilted his head, and walked away.

Thomas jumped to his feet and brushed the sand off his khaki shorts and royal blue golf shirt. "Hey, if chicken gordon blue has chicken in it, I'll be mighty happy. I'm starved."

"It's called *chicken cordon bleu.*" Claire got to her feet, straightened her hair, and brushed the sand off her flowered sundress. "Thomas, where are we now?"

"I don't know. It seems like some kind of tropical resort. I can't believe we're actually at a *tropical resort*. I never thought we'd end up, you know, at a real tropical resort! This place actually looks like one. Except people at tropical resorts don't speak funny languages, do they?" Thomas thought for a moment. "Actually, Matthew wasn't speaking a funny language, although I admit I didn't understand what he was saying half the time. So, in answer to your question, I don't know where we are, but I kinda like it."

"Hey, what's this thing?" asked Claire, showing Thomas the yellow band on her wrist. "Do you have one, too?"

"Yeah. What's it for?"

"I don't know. Maybe it means we're allowed to be here or something."

"Cool! Well, let's go check out that village thing," said Thomas.

"Villa," corrected Claire.

They walked along the beach and noticed that everyone playing volleyball wore a yellow wristband. By the time they reached their villa, they were hot.

The villa was like a large cabin with a wraparound veranda and thatched roof. They climbed the steps to the veranda and saw a swinging chair for two people beside a white-framed screen door. They crossed the veranda, opened the door, and went inside.

It was beautiful. A spiral staircase led to a second floor loft. The living room ceiling was open to the rafters and a bank of tall windows displayed the ocean and sandy beach. There were three comfy U-shaped couches with over-stuffed cushions in front of a huge television screen. In front of the TV was a remote control and instructions for accessing a library of movies.

"Wow! This is fabulous!" he gasped, taking in the size of the TV. "This is going to be awesome! Totally awe— some!" He shook his head in disbelief. "Claire, come and take a look at this!"

Claire had wandered to the kitchen and opened the fridge. "Thomas, you won't believe this!" she called out. "This kitchen is full of food!"

"No way! You know, I like this place more all the time!"

They walked down the hall and found two bedrooms, each with their own bathroom. Each bathroom had a whirlpool bathtub and sauna.

Thomas flopped on his bed. "This is soooo nice!"

"I know what you mean," agreed Claire, who was opening drawers in the dresser in her room. She grinned at the selection of shorts, tops, and sundresses in her closet. "Thomas, take a look inside your closet!"

Thomas clambered off the bed and opened the closet door. It was full of clothes. Clothes that were his size. There were bathing suits and bathrobes and golf shirts and shorts.

"Wow, there's everything I could ever want in here," he shouted to Claire.

"Same here!"

Claire discovered a hairbrush in a cellophane wrapper on her dressing table. She removed the wrapper, then sat in front of the mirror and began to brush her tangled hair.

Thomas went back to the living room.

"Let's check out this spiral staircase," he suggested, running up the stairs. Claire put down the brush and joined him in the loft.

They discovered a spacious room with exercise equipment on one side and shelves on the other, full of board games and books. Near the shelves sat a card table and two comfortable chairs.

"I'll want to spend some time here," smiled Claire, eyeing the collection of books.

"Me too," agreed Thomas, trying out the treadmill.

Hearing a knock at the door, they hurried down the stairs to see who was there. Two dark-haired women in long white dresses held wide trays covered with various round silver lids.

"Heere eze your dinnar," said one of the ladies.

"Thank you!" exclaimed Thomas, rubbing his hands together. He took a tray and darted to the kitchen. The women left after Claire took her tray. She walked to the kitchen, enjoying the aromas wafting up from the food.

Thomas removed the silver lids. The large lid had chicken cordon bleu underneath. Another lid had tossed salad. Another had sautéed baby carrots. Another, baked potatoes. Another had chocolate fudge cake. Another had warm, freshly-baked buns.

"Unbelievable! Unbelievable!" squealed Thomas, unwrapping cutlery from a rolled-up napkin. "I could stay here for weeks!"

"Yeah, this is incredible!" agreed Claire.

Thomas was just about to dig in when there was another knock at the door. Claire could see that a fire wouldn't keep Thomas from eating his supper first, so she went to find out who it was.

A young man stood there. He was wearing white pants, a white dress shirt, and a white baseball hat. He had a neatly trimmed black moustache, a clipboard in his hands, and bowed slightly as he introduced himself.

"Hello, I am Manuel, this week's Outdoor Activities Officer. Tomorrow morning, we are offering parasailing and I wonder if you would be interested in giving it a go?"

"You baht!" called Thomas from the kitchen, his mouth full of baby carrots. He swallowed and walked to the door. "You bet! What time and where?"

"We'll be meeting at the central pier, which is just beside the marina along the boardwalk. We start at

9:00 a.m." Manuel looked at Claire to see if she was interested.

"I think I'll just watch this time," she said.

"Thank you," said Manuel as he wrote something on his clipboard, bowed, turned, and walked across the veranda.

Suddenly, Thomas became concerned. "Uh, Manuel?" he called.

Manuel stopped on the stairs. "Yes?"

"Uh, how much does it, you know, cost to parasail?"

"Like everything else, sir, it is all included. There is no additional expense." He turned and continued on his way.

"Cool." Turning to Claire, Thomas exclaimed, "What's with you? Why didn't you sign up? Parasailing is awesome and it usually costs a ton of money. And here it's free. Free! You'd love it. You hang from a parachute while a motorboat pulls you through the air. It's fantastic!"

"How do you know it's fantastic?" countered Claire. "You've never done it before!"

"I just know it is! You've gotta try it!"

Claire returned to her supper. "I think I'll just watch this time," she repeated.

* * *

There was a crowd of people by the pier at nine o'clock the next morning, but Thomas arrived before everyone else. He was first to parasail. A man helped him into a body harness, making adjustments so it fit snugly. He explained some safety procedures to Thomas while the parachute was spread out along the beach. A gentle breeze filled the parachute as four people held it off the ground. A long cable connected Thomas' harness to a motorboat.

"Ready?" asked the man.

"Ready!"

The man signalled the motorboat driver. As the boat moved out into the bay, the cable tightened and the parachute filled with air. Thomas took only two steps before he rose into the air, his legs still moving. He slowly gained altitude until he was thirty meters above the water.

"Totally awesome!" he shouted.

From the air, Thomas could see they were on an enormous island. There were palm trees everywhere, and clear blue-green ocean surrounded white beaches as far as the eye could see. The ride lasted almost ten minutes, but to Thomas it seemed like thirty seconds. The boat slowed and he gently drifted to the beach, landing softly on the sand.

After the attendant helped him out of his harness, Thomas ran along the shore to find Claire.

"You gotta get in line, Claire. You'd love it!"

"Actually, I found out that horseback riding is happening tomorrow. I'm going to do that. You should come, too, Thomas. You might enjoy it."

"Not a chance," he said. "Last time I went horseback riding, I almost got bucked off. Remember? At Hartley's farm last summer? Remember?"

"That's because you kicked the horse in the wrong place."

"No thanks." He sat down on a bench.

Claire sat beside him. "Thomas?"

"What?"

"I read a sign at the place where you went parasailing and it said you have to be sixteen to do it."

"Yeah? What about it?"

"You're only eleven."

"I'm almost twelve."

"How did you end up parasailing?"

221

"Look, I'm big for my age, okay? I'm probably as big as most sixteen-year-olds."

"You are not!" argued Claire.

"I am so! Uncle Steve said so last summer."

"He says stuff like that every time he sees you." Claire frowned and turned away. "Did you tell them you were sixteen?"

"Listen, Claire, nobody asked, alright?" Thomas stood to his feet. "It doesn't matter. I never got hurt and everything's fine. Okay? Anyway, let's go play some volleyball."

After an hour of playing volleyball with three families from Europe, the morning air was becoming hot.

"Let's get a drink at our villa," suggested Claire.

"Actually I was thinking it must be almost time for lunch."

"It's not even the middle of the morning. You didn't have breakfast that long ago."

"Well, how about a midmorning snack to keep us going until lunch?"

Thomas and Claire found that the villa had been cleaned while they were gone. The dishes in the sink were washed and put away. The beds were made and clothes hung up. The villa looked like it had when they'd first arrived.

Thomas opened the fridge door. It took him a moment to decide which drink he wanted. He chose a strawberry guava sensation. Then he went through several kitchen cupboards until he found what he was searching for: cookies. He opened a bag of oatmeal fudge creams and poured them onto a plate, grabbed his drink, and sprawled on a couch in the living room.

"Let's finish watching that movie we started last night," he said to Claire, turning on the TV. "By the way, why did you turn it off before it was over?"

"You fell asleep on the couch. I woke you up and told you to go to bed, which you did. The movie wasn't very good anyway."

"What do you mean 'it wasn't very good'? *Aliens Raid Antarctica* is a classic! I heard they're coming out with a sequel next year." Thomas munched a cookie.

"Let me guess what it's called," Claire moaned. "*Aliens Raid the Arctic?*"

"Very funny. The sequel is going to be *Aliens Raid Alberta.*" Thomas stuffed another cookie in his mouth. "They're filming it in Alberta or someplace like Alberta. It's based on a true story, you know."

Claire shook her head and sighed. She climbed the spiral staircase and rummaged through the bookcase until she found a paperback from the *Cherise and Tamara* series, about two teenage girls who end up working in a fast-food restaurant in Hollywood. She got herself comfortable and began reading, oblivious to the explosions coming from the TV below her.

At lunchtime, Thomas wasn't that hungry so he only ate a couple of microwaved pizza pops. Claire ate a salad and spent the rest of the afternoon on the veranda reading her book. Thomas watched two more movies: *Revenge of the Mastodons* and *Hardware Store Bloopers.*

Around five o'clock in the afternoon, Matthew came by with the options for supper. Thomas chose the roast beef with Yorkshire pudding, baked red potatoes, and garden peas. Claire chose crepe suzette with fresh berries and cream.

Before Matthew left, Thomas asked Claire, "What's a crate suzappe?"

"It's called *crepe suzette.* It's a thin pancake—it's a kind of dessert."

"No kidding. Hey, Matthew, could I have that as well as the roast beef meal?"

Matthew nodded. "Certainly."

* * *

After supper, Manuel came up the stairs of the villa and knocked on the door.

"And how are you this evening?" he asked.

"Fine," said Claire.

"Full!" sighed Thomas, lying on the couch.

"Tomorrow morning we're offering horseback riding along the beach. Does this interest either of you?"

"Yes, I'll be there," said Claire. "Oh, by the way, are there any age restrictions for horseback riding?"

"No, there aren't. But if you are twelve or younger, you will ride in a corral adjacent to the football field." Manuel could see Thomas lying on the couch. "Thomas, would you like to go horseback riding?"

"Nah, I'll pass. Anything else going on? That parasailing was sure cool."

"Windsurfing lessons will be offered the day after tomorrow."

"Yeah, maybe I'll do that. I'll see."

"And to give you plenty of notice," continued Manuel, "we are organizing a football match for all of our guests in the east playing field by the clubhouse. The game will be this coming Saturday. The floodlights will be on. It should prove to be a delightful experience."

"Do you mean soccer?" asked Claire.

"Yes. Yes, indeed. Soccer. Come and join the fun anytime between seven and nine o'clock. Refreshments and fireworks will follow the game."

"Thank you," said Claire.

* * *

The days passed one after the other, somehow blending together so it was hard to remember on which day a particular thing had happened. Thomas and Claire joined in the Saturday evening soccer game. The air was pleasantly cool as they returned to their villa later that evening.

"Weren't those fireworks amazing?" said Claire as they strolled along.

"Yeah, almost as good as the refreshments. I don't think I've ever seen so many different types of goodies. Those ones with white chocolate and maraschino cherries were really filling. I'm stuffed. It's a good thing we played soccer *before* we ate."

Thomas walked up onto the veranda and sat down on the swinging bench. Claire sat beside him. They could see the light of the moon reflecting off the gently lapping waves in the bay. The palm trees beside their villa shimmered in the warm breeze.

"Thomas," said Claire, breaking the silence.

"Yeah?"

"I don't know exactly how long we've been here. Not very long, but it somehow seems a lot longer."

"Yeah. It's been fabulous!"

There was another pause. "Why do you think we ended up here?"

"Huh? What do you mean?"

"Well, I've been thinking. It seems that everywhere we've been with the Transporter we learned something. And it wasn't until we learned something that we left and went to the next place. What do you think we might have to learn here?"

"I don't know. I'd rather be here than most of those other places. Some of them were pretty scary, if you ask me. Like that place with the bombs exploding all around us. That was real scary!"

"True, but—"

"But what?" asked Thomas as he leaned back on the swing, his hands behind his head.

"I don't know. I mean this place is nice and everything. But—"

"But what? What are you trying to say? Haven't you enjoyed horseback riding and kayaking? You've done both of them two or three times. When do you ever get to do those things? How often do you get to go horseback riding along a beach? And for free?"

"I know. It has been fun. And we're treated really well and everything."

"No kidding. The food has been incredible." Thomas squirmed. "I hope we don't have to learn anything, if it means we'd have to leave. I don't want to learn something and then go. I like it here."

Claire sighed. "I think this place is great, but I guess I'm ready to go. I'd really like it if we went home." There was another long pause. "Do you miss Mom and Dad?"

Thomas crossed his arms and stretched his legs. "Yeah," he said, sighing. "Yeah, I do. I bet they miss us. We've been gone a long time. Maybe they think we've been kidnapped or something. I wonder how much ransom someone would ask for us? Where do you think Mom and Dad would come up with the money? Do you think—"

"Thomas, are you happy here?"

Thomas turned away from Claire a little. "Am I happy? What a dumb question! Of course I'm happy!" He turned back to her and, raising one hand after the other, exclaimed, "I can do anything I want, eat anything I want, sleep in as long as I want. I don't have any chores, I don't have any responsibilities. This is a dream come true!"

"Ever since we left the driveway at home, it's been like a dream - one very long, strange dream."

Thomas frowned. "Aren't you happy?"

Claire took a deep breath as she gazed at the glittering stars. "Do you remember what it was like in that refugee camp?"

Thomas scowled. "I wish I couldn't. That was awful!"

"I was terribly uncomfortable there," said Claire. "I was scared. But it was somehow... satisfying."

Thomas was dumbfounded. "What? Really? You're nuts! How could it have possibly been satisfying?"

Claire was quiet for a moment, then continued. "It was satisfying because we helped people. I began to realize how I take things for granted. Now here, we're terribly comfortable, but... but I'm not feeling very satisfied."

"What on earth are you talking about?"

"It's fun here and everything. This kind of life is okay. But not forever. The first few days were very nice. I've really enjoyed it, but I'm ready to do something else. I'm ready to do something useful. It's time to go. I want to go home." She looked Thomas in the eyes. "How long do you think we should stay here?"

"Well, that's not up to us. We can't go anywhere without the Transporter, and we haven't even found parts of it yet. It'll turn up eventually. Always has. Don't worry. Besides, when we leave, we have no idea where we'll go. You know that. But I do know where I'm going right now. I'm tired. I'm going to bed!"

Thomas stood abruptly and marched into the villa.

Claire stayed for a while, gently swinging back and forth, watching the light of the moon sparkle on the distant waves.

* * *

A few more days went by. The last two days, Thomas had requested hot dogs for supper. He and Claire played some board games, but never seemed to finish them. Thomas went parasailing again, but it wasn't quite as exciting as the first time. Claire didn't ask him how it went.

The next day, after watching parts of three movies, Thomas went for a swim in the Olympic-sized pool beside the marina while Claire walked along the beach. After swimming, Thomas sat in the hot tub for a while, then thought he'd get something to eat back at the villa. He asked the lifeguard where the towels were and was directed to a table near the pool.

When Thomas lifted a towel to dry himself, he uncovered the Transporter. He was shocked. He quickly wrapped it in his towel and hurried back to the villa, hoping he would get there before Claire returned from her walk. He hid the Transporter under his bed, then ran to the couch and opened a magazine just as Claire walked in.

"How was your swim, Thomas?"

"Oh fine, fine. Yes, it was nice. Very nice. Thank you. Yep."

Claire stared at him. "Thomas, are you alright?"

"Me? Yes, I'm fine. Uh-huh. How was your walk?"

"Refreshing. I was able to sort some things out in my mind." She looked sideways at him as he got up and walked to the kitchen.

"Great. Anyway, I'm just going to get a bite and head over to the, uh... the, uh... tennis court. Yep. The tennis court. So, I guess I'll see you later."

"Thomas, are you sure you're alright?"

"Couldn't be better," he said, grabbing three ice cream sandwiches from the freezer and scurrying out the door. "Catch you later!"

Claire watched him run along the trail to the tennis court. Walking back into the living room, she picked up her *Cherise and Tamara* book, the second in the series, climbed the spiral staircase to the loft, and put it back on the shelf. She had only read half of it.

* * *

The next day, Thomas took more windsurfing lessons in the morning, then spent the afternoon kayaking back and forth in the bay near the shore. He hadn't returned by the time Matthew came by to take their supper orders. "Tonight we have filet mignon with Asian rice, cucumber salad, and—"

"Excuse me, Matthew," interrupted Claire. "Would there happen to be any soup for supper?"

"Soup?"

"Yes."

"Yes, we do have soup available. We have… shrimp bisque, vichyssoise, French onion…"

"Could we have two bowls of chicken noodle soup with crackers, please?"

"Chicken noodle soup? Certainly. Anything else?"

"No. That's all. Thank you."

Thomas appeared just as the supper lady arrived. There was only one tray of food.

"Did you order for me, Claire?" Thomas asked.

"Yes, I did."

Thomas looked around. "Where's the other tray?"

"I think everything is here," she explained, taking the tray from the lady. "Thank you very much."

The lady bowed and silently returned down the veranda stairs.

"What's for supper?" Thomas asked.

"Chicken noodle soup," answered Claire as she set the tray on the kitchen table.

"What?"

Claire placed a bowl of soup in front of him. "Chicken noodle soup. Just like Mom makes."

"No one makes chicken noodle soup as good as Mom," clarified Thomas, trying a spoonful. "Ummm, not bad, not bad."

"Thomas?" said Claire as she crushed some crackers into her soup, "do you have anything you want to tell me?"

Thomas hesitated. "Uh, sure. I can't windsurf worth beans, but I can kayak pretty good. I can't play tennis at all, but I'm pretty good at ping-pong."

"Anything else?"

Thomas stopped his spoon just before it reached his mouth. He looked off to the side without moving his head. He swallowed. "Like... like what?"

"Like this," said Claire as she walked across the kitchen, opened a cupboard door, and took out the Transporter. She put it on the kitchen table.

Thomas swallowed again. "Where did that thing come from?" he asked innocently.

Claire stared straight at him, then raised an eyebrow.

"You shouldn't go snooping under other people's beds!" he snapped, sounding angry.

"I didn't snoop under your bed."

"Well, where did you get it from then?"

"I saw it on top of your bed when I came home. I gather you put it under your bed?"

"I never said I did."

"Well, who did then?"

"Well, who put it on top of my bed?"

"Probably the cleaning staff," answered Claire quickly. Her eyes narrowed and she pressed her lips together.

Thomas continued eating his soup.

"How long have you had it, Thomas? Why didn't you tell me?"

Thomas stopped eating and put down his spoon. "I don't know. Not that long. I found it yesterday, I think. Or the day before. I don't remember. Anyway, let's talk about it tomorrow after we've had a good night's sleep." Then he mumbled, "Once you've calmed down a little..."

"No, I want to talk about it now! We've been through so much together and now I feel like you've tricked me,

Thomas! Again! How could you do that?" Thomas looked down at his soup as Claire continued. "We just went through this at Mount Everest with the allegedly lost eggbeater. How could you do it again?"

Thomas squirmed in his chair and fidgeted with his hands. He cleared his throat. "I didn't want us to leave," he said quietly. He looked around the room. "I like it here!"

"Do you really? You don't finish watching the movies you start. You don't even finish the hot dogs you order. Don't you miss being at home? How much longer do you really want to stay here? Another day? A week? Forever? What about Mom and Dad?"

Thomas took a deep breath and was quiet for a long time. Tears flowed down his cheeks. "I guess I've been kinda selfish." He cleared his throat again. "I'm... sorry, Claire. I'm sorry. I really am!"

The ocean breeze gently shook the blinds in the living room.

Claire sighed. "I forgive you. Again."

Thomas smiled a little and sniffed. "Thanks. Again." He scratched his ear. "You know, it's almost like I forget everything I learn." He looked out the window toward the ocean. "It's just like Dad says all the time."

"What's that?"

"How does that saying go?" he asked. "Oh yeah. Most unhappiness..." He stopped talking, and gazed at the ceiling, even though his lips kept moving.

They continued together in unison, speaking slowly: "Most unhappiness in the world is caused by giving up what you want *most* for what you want at the *moment*."

"Yeah, that's it," said Thomas.

"So, what do you want *most*?" asked Claire.

Thomas stared at his empty bowl of soup. "I want to go home."

"Really?"

"Yeah, really. Even surrounded by all this luxury, I want to be home."

"What happens if the Transporter doesn't take us home?"

"I know. I still want to go. Maybe it'll be home this time."

Neither said anything for a long time. The waves in the bay broke gently along the shore.

"Should we leave now?" Claire asked.

"Sure," Thomas said with a nod. "But promise me something."

"What's that?"

"Promise me that whenever you see me being selfish or stupid, you'll remind me about it."

"I will. And you'll tell me, too?"

Thomas smiled. "Sure."

He picked up the Transporter as Claire put her hand on his shoulder. He pushed the Activator and immediately they felt the warm ocean air rushing past them as they spun head over heels. A faint high-pitched siren sound blended with the sound of rushing air.

It became dark and the spinning went on for a very long time. They both began to feel dizzy.

Eventually, the spinning slowed and finally stopped, until they were just floating through the air. Gradually, the air around them became brighter. Claire could see something that looked familiar. It was their house. Thomas could make out the shape of the garage.

Slowly, they descended until they softly landed feet first just outside the garage door. They stared at each other for a long moment. A few seconds later, the Transporter landed beside them and bounced onto the grass. One of the eggbeaters broke off and rolled along the concrete driveway.

Their mother poked her head out the back door of the house. "How many times do I have to call you two for lunch?" she asked. "Your soup is getting cold!"

She slipped back inside the door.

Thomas and Claire looked at each other, then started to laugh. They both had big grins and Claire had a tear in her eye. They hugged each other and didn't let go for a long time.

"Claire?" Thomas said as he walked over to pick up the Transporter.

"Yes?"

"Let's go eat! I'm starved!"

Discussion Questions

What did you like best about the resort?

Was it alright for Thomas to go parasailing even though he wasn't old enough?

What are Claire's reasons for wanting to leave the resort?

Claire forgave Thomas a second time (first at the end of Chapter 12, and then at the end of this chapter). Do you think she should have? What might happen to their relationship if Thomas deceives her again in the future?

After all of their experiences and adventures, what do you think Thomas and Claire's relationship will be like now compared with when Claire first came into the garage in Chapter 1?

CPSIA information can be obtained at www.ICGtesting.com
Printed in the USA
LVOW04s0322091214

417841LV00010B/34/P